Get Away by Bike

Get Away by Bike

The Essential Guide for Every Cycle Tourist

Les Woodland

PELHAM BOOKS
Stephen Greene Press

PELHAM BOOKS/Stephen Greene Press

Published by the Penguin Group
27 Wrights Lane, London W8 5TZ, England
Viking Penguin Inc., 40 West 23rd Street, New York, New York 10010, USA
The Stephen Greene Press Inc., 15 Muzzey Street, Lexington, Massachusetts 02173, USA
Penguin Books Australia Ltd, Ringwood, Victoria, Australia
Penguin Books Canada Ltd, 2801 John Street, Markham, Ontario, Canada L3R 1B4
Penguin Books (NZ) Ltd, 182–190 Wairau Road, Auckland 10, New Zealand

Penguin Books Ltd, Registered Offices: Harmondsworth, Middlesex, England

First published 1990

Typeset in Linotron 10.5/12 Ehrhardt by
Cambrian Typesetters, Frimley, Surrey
Printed and bound in Great Britain by
Butler & Tanner Ltd, Frome and London

A CIP catalogue record for this book is available from the British Library

ISBN 0 7207 1921 6

To Tom and the 'B' for putting up with a coarse and rowdy young lad

Acknowledgements

Unless otherwise credited, the photographs have been kindly supplied by Cyclographic Publications.

Contents

II COUNTRY BY COUNTRY

The entries for each country include sections on Language,
Accommodation, Cycling, Weather, Public transport, Maps,
Useful addresses, Currency and Other details

III YOUR BICYCLE

I. The Great Escape

1. A Certain Dull Ache

Whenever you read about cycling, you can bet your life on two things. The first is that the words have been written by a sun-darkened veteran with eyes locked half-closed against the horizon. The second is that they won't once mention that you can come home from a bike ride feeling absolutely cream-crackered.

Well, this isn't one of those books. You're dealing now with a man who's known the weakening of spirit, who knows what it's like to sleep in a church doorway for lack of the strength to continue. And you're in the company of a man who knows what it's like to wake with an ache like church bells at midnight. When in the next few hundred pages you sense I'm getting too enthusiastic, I ask you to remember that, like an advertiser's disclaimer, I want my gravestone shaped like a worn-out rain cape and engraved with the words: 'He only meant what was best'.

I've split this book in an unusual way. The bit that you might think would come first – the section on buying a bike – is the last. So far as I'm concerned, the most important decision isn't the kind of bike you intend to ride but the decision to go cycling in the first place. And that's where I'm starting. After all, it's as bad to choose a skittish Tour de France kitten-bike for a first ride as it is to circle the world on a small-wheeled shopper. Leave that choice until later; for the moment, start on whatever you've got.

Two-thirds or more of the western world lives in a built-up area. In many places, the proportion is growing. We like being together. That's convenient enough for public transport, employment, shopping and finding cinemas which show obscure French films, but it doesn't do much for bike riding.

You have, in short, to prepare your escape plan. You have to get out of the suburbs, because the best cycling's to be had in the country. Now, there's no universal plan for this. Getting out of Derry and Derby is relatively straightforward, because they're not big places. Escaping from the centre of London or Birmingham is altogether different.

There are three ways of doing it.

GETTING AWAY BY BIKE

A few enlightened towns have built a network of cycle routes. Three cheers for you if you live in Peterborough, Harlow or Stevenage. Two and a half cheers if

It can be a long ride through city streets to get to the lanes, but a train, a canal towpath or even back streets might make it more pleasant.

it's Cambridge or Milton Keynes, where the spirit was willing but the flesh proved weak.

Thankfully, even the worst of the modern set-ups are better than their 1920s counterparts, which have now all but disappeared. They shadowed main roads where they were safest and then threw cyclists out unprotected into junctions where the danger was greatest. Sadly, even modern paths don't share the priority of the roads that they follow, so you'll find yourself repeatedly giving way to traffic approaching from behind and opting to cross your path. This isn't a happy situation and, if you don't find yourself more at ease on the road itself, you'll just have to put up with it.

Note, though, that it's not obligatory in Britain to use a cycle path. It takes special legislation to make a path obligatory. You have the option of using whichever route has the better surface, and whichever is least obstructed (in some towns, cycle paths are regarded as convenient car parks and milk float routes).

Cycle paths (not tracks, please, which are racing circuits) are shown by blue signs, usually circular, displaying an old-fashioned, white bicycle. It's one of the standardized European traffic symbols and you'll find it all over the Continent. There's a slight distinction between the circular and the rectangular version, but the circular version is so dominant that by the time you come across a rectangular one you'll have forgotten the difference anyway.

Chances are, though, that you won't have a cycle route escape. And now a little ingenuity is necessary. Look, for example, at street maps and their Ordnance Survey equivalent. You might not find a quiet route but you might find a quieter one. Look for runs of housing streets, paths across public parks, canal towpaths, and anything else that makes your life comfortable. Remember, too, that an early start reduces the traffic dramatically, especially on Sundays.

Campaign groups can often help by suggesting good routes, and they might welcome your advice as well. Most towns have a group of some sort, often associated with the Cyclists Touring Club, Friends of the Earth, or some regional body. You can get the address of your local one by contacting the Cycle Campaign Network at Tress House, Stamford Street, London SE1 (01–928 7220) or the Cyclists Touring Club at Cotterell House, 69 Meadrow, Godalming, Surrey GU7 3HS (04868–7217).

The CTC's address is particularly useful and the club will get several mentions in the pages to come. The headquarters are on the A3100 between Guildford and Godalming and the office is open to callers from 9 am to 4.30 pm, Monday to Friday, although there's a 24-hour telephone answering service.

BY TRAIN

British Rail are never sure whether they still welcome cyclists. In 1898, 50,000 cyclists left Waterloo station in London during Easter week alone. More recently, the CTC chartered whole trains, and cyclists in corduroy shorts puffed through the suburbs like casually-dressed scoutmasters. These specials were a great success, but then British Rail demanded high minimum bookings, so the cyclists' specials hit the buffers.

For many years BR charged by the mile for accompanied bikes. Then they switched to asking for half the adult fare. And then, on 1 June 1977, they ended bike fares of any kind, after years of badgering by the CTC. Bikers could hardly believe their luck. But things went too well.

The trains attracted not only weekend cyclists with sandwich boxes and saddlebags but thousands of pin-stripers who realized they could dodge car park charges and Underground fares if they took their roadsters on commuter services. According to BR, this upsurge in custom clogged up the guard's van and delayed the trains. Then BR, having mistakenly forecast that rail traffic would fall rather than rocket, made things worse by reducing the baggage area in their high-speed and lightweight suburban trains.

The problem now is that the position is neither one thing nor the other. You can take your bike on some of the trains some of the time, on a few of the trains all of the time, and on others not at all. British Rail and the CTC will supply you with a free leaflet called *The British Rail Guide to Biking by Train*, but it's as useless as it is well-meaning. For a start, it's bewilderingly complicated, and it takes into account neither local exceptions and changes of train-type, nor the fact that many station staff don't themselves know what the rules are. So, for all that the new rules say you might have to book at least ten minutes before departure, it's a matter of great debate at stations whether that means ten minutes before the train leaves an individual station or ten minutes before it left wherever it began its journey.

As the CTC said in its magazine, *Cycletouring*, in August 1987, the future 'is certainly not something to contemplate with any satisfaction. The present situation [in which bookable trains will take no more than two bicycles] is unacceptable to families or groups – ironically, the users who stood to gain most from the 1977 free offer . . . It may be significant that around a dozen stands at the recent Olympia cycle show included some sort of fold-down bike.' Folding bikes aren't classified as bicycles by British Rail's reckoning and can be taken free and without reservations.

All I can do is urge you to ring or, better still, visit your nearest station as long before your journey as possible. There are restrictions too on:

– High Speed Trains (125s), especially during the week and particularly on the line from King's Cross to Scotland
– suburban trains in and out of London, especially in the direction of the rush hour each morning and evening
– the lightweight Sprinter and Pacer trains which now operate many services, particularly the diagonal route from Essex to Manchester and Liverpool
– some lightweight electric services, notably from Bedford to London
– all boat trains from London to Folkestone and Dover (although see the chapter on cycling abroad)
– trains on the Isle of Wight, London Underground and Vale of Rheidol steam services.

Some long journeys are impossible to make because of a combination of restrictions.

Despite all the problems – keeping other people's timetables, going miles to find the station, and coping with occasionally awkward staff – I prefer taking a bike by train to taking it by car. Nearly all long-distance trains and all but the smallest stations have somewhere to wash and change, and the best stations supply tea and buns as well. If not, there's usually a café nearby.

If your train requires a booking, you can make it at any station, whether it's on the route or not. You can also make it at BR-accredited travel agents. The booking fee – £3 in 1989 – covers any number of trains in a day. But obviously it covers specific trains, so you've got problems if your train runs late and misses the connection. In addition to your passenger ticket, you'll get a similar one for your bike. Make sure that written on it are the details of the trains you have reserved because, curiously, the guard rarely knows about the bookings and your ticket is the only evidence you have.

Tie a label to the bike, mark it with the destination station and changing points. Some regions insist on the label, others never ask, but it's good for peace of mind. Never assume the guard will be at the back of the train, nor that the guard's van you spot first is the one you want. There's usually more than one, and on Sprinters there's one at each end, although one end is occupied by the drinks trolley. It is best to wait three-quarters of the way towards the back end of the platform; you'll spot the right guard's van as it passes. And with luck, the guard will see you and open the doors.

Do all you can to place the bike in the luggage van yourself. For all their occupational grumpiness, most guards are careful. But there are exceptions. Lean the bike against the carriage wall or the security fencing, and fix it with an elasticated strap. Never lock the bike to the carriage. If you do, several tons of mail will arrive later and the guard, unable to move your machine, will smother it in bills and junk mail.

Be careful on Sundays to check that your train back will run when the timetable says it will. Sunday is engineering day and the railway runs to whims of its own. Note that when British Rail say: 'Passengers and their luggage will be transferred by a special road service', they mean a bus – and they won't take your bike, booked or otherwise.

Finally, never consign an unaccompanied bicycle to British Rail, unless it's with the unavoidable exception of registered baggage on Continental routes. The cost in 1989 was £8.05 with a railcard or ticket, £12.08 without one. I don't doubt the service is efficient; I note, though, that the bike goes 'at owner's risk'.

BY CAR

The remaining option, since coaches won't take bikes, is to go by car. You just stow your bike and drive off into the countryside. And there you park and ride around to your heart's content. Usually you can get straight to the centre of the area you want to explore, although if that countryside happens to be the Peaks or another big attraction, your parked car will help spoil the very scenery that others want to enjoy.

The snag is that your journey must end where it began. You can only go in a circle. At least by train you can arrive at one station and leave from another – and that could mean a tailwind all the way.

There's no easy way to take a bike by car. You put it either inside or outside. Inside is better and safer, but it's got to come to bits. The mudguards and handlebars may be awkward to stow. The mudguards might well get bent enough to distort for good. You might, with a hatchback, be able to collapse the back seats, remove the front or perhaps both wheels, and inch the machine into place. Once it fits, remember how you did it.

Slightly simpler is to strap the bike to the roof-rack. You've probably seen cyclists carrying their bikes vertically. They do it that way because it scratches neither the bike nor the car. Turn the bike upside down and place the handlebars on the front rung of the rack. If the saddle now happens to rest on another rung, then things are going well. If not, you'll have to slide the bike backwards and forwards until you've found a compromise. With dropped handlebars, for instance, you could strap either the flat tops of the bars or the handholds of the brakes. It all depends. Don't strap the saddle straight to the rack or you'll end up with a damaged saddle. You'll get a dent in the leather or other 'hard' saddle and maybe even a tear in a soft-surfaced mattress one. And if you've got one of those hard saddles with a stuck-on chamois cover, the wringing motion might loosen the surface almost imperceptibly. Imperceptibly, that is, until you start to feel your saddle sores. Instead, place a sponge or a roll of newspaper between metal and saddle.

Strap the bike firmly. There's nothing better than straps with roller buckles, the sort that you'd use for pedals with toeclips. The more straps the better. Tighten them all, then re-tighten them, then check the securing bolts on the roof-rack itself. A bike sticks up a long way and it acts as a powerful lever. Therefore any slackness in the attachment is exaggerated.

If you think the worst happens only to the inexperienced, I'm afraid you're wrong. It wasn't that long ago that a bunch of professionals were travelling to a distant race and had all four bikes come adrift, complete with the roof-rack, as they spurted up the M1 motorway. The whole lot – say nearly £3,000 of equipment – crashed to the ground. It was ruined. And yet it could have been worse; it might have fallen into the path of following cars and caused a terrible accident.

Frankly, events like that are thankfully rare. But there are other risks. Once the bike's on the rack, you can no longer see it. I once rode 80 miles into a headwind to recover a car parked in the Norfolk town of Hunstanton. Grateful that my ordeal was over, I lashed the bike into place and sat in the driver's seat. I started the engine . . . and drove obliviously towards the hanging bar that prevented overnight parking by commercial vehicles. Without the bike, the car entered the car park easily; with it, it left only with a clanging crash which bent the front forks. You have been warned!

You can, just about, get four bikes on a decent roof-rack. They have to have dropped handlebars, though – dropped bars being narrower than straight ones. You do it by alternating the bikes, the first leading with the handlebars, the second with the saddle, and so on. It's harder with straight handlebars because everything gets tangled up, but you should be able to get three in place. Three's a safer number, anyway, and two gives even more security of mind.

Several firms make roof-rack attachments which will do away with bodged-up jobs with toestraps. Caratti's, for example, holds the bike upright by the front forks and the rear wheel rim. You carry the front wheel separately or strap it to the bike. Write to them at Unit 15, Walker Way, Thornbury Trading Estate,

Bristol BS12 2US (0454–411701), and they'll send you a list of stockists. A similar rack is made by D and P Dixon, of 29 Marine Close, Leigh-on-Sea, Essex SS9 2RE. Rather simpler is a gadget made by Tag. It holds the bike in the same way, but you buy just the attachments and use your own roof-rack. Tag supply directly from 12 Carlton Way, Cambridge CB4 1XN and through dealers.

When you look for a dealer, by the way, look for the crucial words: 'lightweight specialist'. It tells as much about the owner's frame of mind as it does about his stock.

You may prefer to consider a rear-mounting carrier. The bike is supported vertically behind the boot, set sideways. Most carriers support two bikes. A set-up like this reduces wind resistance, of course, and you might feel happier seeing what it is that you're carrying, and that the bikes are still in place. On the other hand, the machines stop you getting at whatever you're carrying in the boot. And they make the car back-heavy, of course. There are also regulations about what is allowed to protrude from the otherwise smooth outline of a car body, and how much you're allowed to stick on the car astern of the lights. That's not to say they're not a good buy. It's just that there are questions to ask of the distributors. Among the makers are Fel, of 42 Woodlands Avenue, Emsworth, Hampshire PO10 7QE (0243–373894), and Adams Engineering, of Moreland Street, Nottingham NG2 3GQ (0602–865421).

2. A Bicycle, the Humble Mayfly, and You (Some Golden Rules)

No one has found a more efficient way of travelling than by bike. Weight for weight, that is. It uses a lot less energy per mile than walking, and unbelievably less than a jumbo jet. Even the humble mayfly, which lives only a few hours and feels middle-aged by lunchtime, uses more energy than a cyclist.

That doesn't mean, though, that it's a good idea to get on your bike and race off towards the horizon without some planning. If you haven't ridden a bike much lately, you'll find there are nasty surprises. You sit on a very soft bit of your body, for example, and it will bruise. Also, all the little arterioles and veins through your legs may not be up to it. Next day you might be walking around like a worn-out rugby forward. But it doesn't have to be that way. So here come the golden rules of cycling.

RIDE LITTLE BUT FREQUENTLY

Cycling's a fitness sport, just like jogging, lacrosse and blow-football. You won't do yourself the kind of damage you can get courtesy of a hockey stick, and you won't get ricked as you might in judo. Thanks to the handlebars, saddle and pedals being pretty much fixed commodities, you can't tweak your muscles and joints.

The downside, though, is that the wheels are whacking big gyroscopes and hold you upright even when you might otherwise have fallen over. You can't play netball indefinitely because, long before you sink to your knees, you'll have lost all the skill of getting the ball in the net. Squash players lose their eye for the ball well before they have to be carried off by men in St John Ambulance uniforms. But not with cycling.

You can, if you like, ride a bike until you're reduced to a quivering heap. And the wretched bike will *still* keep you upright. And you *still* have to get home.

The trick, therefore, is to ride little but often. There's a satisfaction to riding 200 miles a day, and the record is rather more than 500. But cycling for pleasure is measured in hours of satisfaction and not in miles. If you have to think of distance, reckon on 25 miles being plenty far enough for an opening 'serious' ride, and only then after several shorter ones.

The more you ride, the more you open all the little blood vessels that carry in the blood, oxygen and sugar. Since physiologists will tell you that fitness is specific to the activity, it follows that any degree of fitness at football, swimming or ballroom dancing will be of limited help with cycling. It'll be *some* help, but it won't get you doing 100 miles in four hours on your first big thrash.

As you ride, you learn all the little skills of cycling. I don't mean balance, road signals and avoiding Spanish refrigerator trucks. I mean the subconscious ironing out of unnecessary extra movements. Your pedalling becomes smooth and relaxed, even when you're climbing a hill. You're at ease, even on fast descents and in heavy traffic. It comes, but only in time.

If you're new to the game, start with five miles, then ten miles, and build it up little by little until you're riding as far in a day as you're happy with. The actual distance doesn't matter; it's the happiness that counts.

Remember that fitness comes in any sport only if you practise it at least three times a week. You'll get better at it with just weekend trips, but you won't get fitter, if you see the distinction.

So why not try riding to work once or twice a week? You will feel a bit strange when you arrive on a bicycle for the first time, but from then on it's a piece of cake. I once rode no small number of miles to a newspaper office where first I was scoffed at; within the month, though, the message was getting through and I was just one of a little army of fellow cyclists. Within three months the publishers had renovated the bike sheds and no one could get in the gents' in the morning for cyclists having a wash and changing their shirts.

If it's just a few miles, ride in the clothes you'll be working in. As the distance increases, so you'll prefer to wear perhaps a tracksuit and have a complete change of clothes at work. The days have gone when folk in tracksuits were curious sights – the fitness boom has seen to that. Drive (or take the bus) once a week and take in all the clothes you need. Or ride in on the first morning with a fully-loaded saddlebag. From then on, you're free of bus schedules, train delays, parking problems and every other curse of the modern commuter.

In many cities, cyclists travel faster than motor traffic anyway. The average traffic speed in London now is just eight mph. It's not necessarily the case, therefore, that cycling will take you longer. If it does, or if you live further from work than you choose to ride, why not drive in to a convenient village or suburb with your bike on the roof-rack and ride the miles that drive you battiest in your car? And if it *does* take a bit longer, so what? Is life really so pressing that you can't afford a bit more time each day, enjoying yourself, feeling better?

That reminds me of Johnny Helms, whose cartoons entertain readers of *Cycling Weekly* and the walkers' magazine *The Great Outdoors*. Johnny was always pushed for time on his way to work. At the end of the day, though, his time was his own and he'd take a longer route. Sometimes he'd stop 15 miles from home and get into conversation:

> 'Yes, sir?' said the landlord of the Spinner and Burgamot.
> 'A pint of bitter, please.'
> I watched with pleasurable anticipation as the liquid swirled and frothed into the glass tankard and then settled into a clear amber liquid that sparkled in the sunlight streaming through the open windows. It tasted as good as it looked and I emptied half the tankard in one long, slow, satisfying draught.
> 'Aaaaah . . . that was good.'
> 'You're cycling, sir?'
> 'Yes, I'm just on the way home from work.'
> 'And where do you work?'
> 'Runcorn.'
> 'That's a long way on a bicycle.'
> (It is, in fact, about 12 miles.)

'And where do you live?'

'Widnes.'

The landlord opened his mouth and then shut it again. He appeared to be confused. Widnes is one mile north of Runcorn, across the River Mersey. The Spinner and Burgamot lies well to the east of both.

'You're not lost, sir?'

A reasonable question from anyone who thinks that travelling is just getting from A to B, or Runcorn to Widnes.

'No, I often come this way.'

Or through Delamere Forest. Or through the serenely quiet villages of Daresbury and Hatton. I use about 20 different routes to and from work. The shortest is five miles and the longest about 40. The Spinner and Burgamot is on the 33-mile route.

It's tempting to see a bike as a way round the drinking laws. True, you can't be breathalysed as a cyclist, but you're still legally and morally bound by the law. It is quite possible to ride when you're drunk but you might not go in a straight line. The drink will go to your legs and make you feel very leaden for the ride home.

But you don't have to get pie-eyed at a pub, and you don't even have to drink alcohol. A ride to a village pub on a summer's evening is a delightful experience, made still sweeter by the knowledge that the exercise is doing you good.

EASY DOES IT

You might have a bike without gears, but the chances are that it does. In fact, bikes with single gears are usually geared fairly low (in other words, more pedal revs to the mile), and bikes with several gears are frequently geared too high.

For the moment, though, you have whatever you've got. Whether it's a hub gear (like a Sturmey-Archer) or a derailleur (like a racing bike), you have the choice of which gear to use. Don't automatically go straight into the highest gear. It's not like driving a car; you don't save energy just because you're revving more slowly. Start in a low gear and work up little by little until you've matched your pedalling to your walking rate. If you'd just amble as you walked, do the cycling equivalent by pushing gently in a higher gear. If you're riding with any purpose, spin along in a lower gear.

Heavy slogging is exhausting. It's uninspiring and it makes your muscles ache. 'Lightweight' pedalling respects your legs and produces the kind of fitness you want. It's tempting to climb on, shove the gear lever to its highest position, and push hard. Nifty pedalling's a skill which you have to learn. That's why it seems easier at first to stab at the pedals.

The other point is to place the ball of your foot and not the instep on the

A gentle ride to a village pub . . . a great way to start (and a pretty good way to continue).

pedal. The instep seems more obvious, but the ball of your foot makes cycling not only kinder to your feet but gives you a little extra push as you flex your ankles. If you've got toeclips fitted to your pedals, you'll have no choice anyway.

SIT COMFORTABLY

Since you're sitting on the thing for quite some time, make sure your bike fits. It's astonishing how many people either don't know or don't care. They must ache with a vengeance.

You touch the bike in five places – twice on the pedals, twice on the handlebars, once on the saddle. It's a once-and-for-all adjustment to make cycling so much happier. Do take the trouble. After all, you wouldn't drive a car without adjusting the seat, and you wouldn't walk in someone else's shoes.

The saddle: It doesn't matter whether it's a padded splendour with coiled springs like an old mattress, or a rock-hard Reg Harris bum-cracker. Check the up-and-down adjustment. Saddles are fitted to a silvery tube called the seat pin by a clamp which grips the pin and the frame of the saddle. The pin is held in the frame by a pinch-bolt in the lug that joins the top tube (which you may know as the cross-bar) and the seat tube (as distinct from the seat pin). On ancient bikes, this pinch-bolt might be a collar, but no matter. It's this bit that has to be adjusted.

Put on shoes without heels and sit on the saddle. Spin the pedals so that the cranks form a straight line with the seat tube. The lower pedal will now be as far from the saddle as it can be. Put your heels on each pedal and pedal gently backwards. If you do this in comfort, the saddle's too low. If you wobble more than gently, it's too high. The trick is to move the saddle up and down until you can just about do it.

You do this by slackening the pinch-bolt (posh frames might have an allen key fitting, others will have an ordinary nut) and pulling the seat pin right out of the frame. You might as well do this because you can then give it a smear of grease where it'll go back in the frame. A jammed seat pin is a pig to get out (as you might just have discovered) and the grease stops it happening again. If it *does* happen, try easing fluid.

You've got to pull it out, anyway, if you plan to raise the saddle. This is for safety's sake. Painful surprises befall those who leave less than two inches of pin inside the frame, and you won't know how long your seat pin is unless you pull it out and look.

What if you're down to the last two inches and you've still got to pull the saddle up further? Well, you can't do it. Not with that seat pin, anyway. If there's just half an inch in it, you might decide it makes no odds. Rather a saddle that's too low than one that falls out of the frame. But more than half an inch and you need to buy a longer seat pin. Take the old one to the bike shop because not only is the length important but the diameter is critical. And here there's a bit of good news. Until the last few years, it was hard to buy a long seat pin. Now, though, we've got a craze for mountain bikes (or ATBs, all-terrain bicycles) which have small frames and long seat pins. The world has never been a happier place for people more than six feet tall.

The problem's simpler the other way round. If your saddle's too high, all you have to do is push more and more seat pin into the frame until it's at the right height. If the whole lot disappears and the saddle's still too high, you're in the same boat as the man who can't buy enough seat pin. There comes a time to concede that your frame's just the wrong size.

The idea of adjusting your saddle height in this odd way (with your heels on the pedals) is that eventually you should be able to put the ball of the foot on each pedal and then nearly but not quite straighten each leg as you ride.

The other check is fore-and-aft adjustment. The saddle's fixed to the pin by a clamp, either two large bolts or an allen key or two small nuts. However it's arranged, see that when the cranks are horizontal and you're sitting comfortably, a plumb line drops from the slight hollow at the back of your knee cap, down through the axle of the forward pedal. Slackening the clamp will let the saddle slide backwards or forwards. In sliding, it might also tilt. Perfection demands a horizontal saddle, with the nose as high as the back (the cantle). If I were re-designing the human body, I'd take away all the nerves where you sit on the saddle. Since I can't, all I can suggest is that you get the saddle either horizontal or with the slightest upward tilt at the nose. Certainly don't tip it down at the front or you'll throw weight on your arms and legs as well as tug at the delicate skin of your backside. You'll also keep sliding down the saddle.

The handlebars are the last setting. Dropped handlebars should have the straight section at the top an inch or two lower than the nose of the saddle. Straight or slightly upturned handlebars should be about the same height as the saddle, but certainly no higher. Bikes go in a straight line because of the caster action of the front wheel, but if you take the weight off the wheel it doesn't work. While it may *seem* safer to raise the handlebars, the truth is the opposite. Distributing your weight like this also makes you lighter in the saddle so that you can use your arm and back muscles as well.

Handlebars are held by a stem, which might have an extension to move them further forward. The length of the extension is fixed and the only way to change it is to buy a new one. The stem is pushed into the fork tube, which is the extension of the front forks which continues up through, and is hidden by, the head tube of the frame. The head tube is the smallest main tube and the one on which most makers put their badge.

Friction isn't enough. The stem has to be wedged into the fork tube and then clamped. You'll find a nut or an allen key in the head of the handlebar stem. Slacken it and the nut will rise from the stem. Let it rise about a third of an inch, cover the nut with a pad and tap it with a hammer, just firmly enough to push the nut back down. The nut is the head of a long rod, threaded at the far end and screwed into a wedge-shaped nut. If you tighten the nut, the wedge rises and pushes out the split ends of the stem, jamming them against the fork tube. If you undo the securing nut too far, the wedge drops off completely, which isn't disastrous but is certainly a nuisance, because you've then got to retrieve it from inside the frame.

Raise or lower the handlebars and re-tighten the stem. If you can't get it to grip straight away, lift the whole rod assembly to jam it enough to get it started. You don't need to tighten any nut on a bike ferociously, by the way – just enough to be sure.

The over-cautious assume that what seems a low handlebar position restricts forward vision. In fact, you get just as good a view of the road from any position, provided you keep your eyes open. Concentration counts more than position.

Weight on the handlebars improves steering and makes sharp braking safer and easier. The arms are already partly stressed to support the body. Your arms, your body and a horizontal line back from the top of the handlebars should form an equilateral triangle. It won't be perfect, but it's the best way. If you grip the inside (vertical bends) of dropped handlebars, your bent elbows should be able to touch your knees at their most forward position. If you're tall, your elbows should just clear your knees.

EQUIP YOURSELF FOR THE WEATHER

Cycling's wonderful most of the time, but it's at its most wonderful when the sun shines. All you need then is a light shirt or blouse and a pair of shorts.

Cobbles can be a pain in more than just your neck. But winter weather's much less of a problem if you dress for it ... although anoraks can make you as wet inside as the weather outside.

In cooler weather, though, you need to exercise more caution. You can ride in almost anything that you'd wear in 'ordinary' life, just as you could wear it to ride a horse or play rugby. But there's better, specialized, clothing, as you might imagine. For further details see pages 37 to 39.

You can buy specialized clothing at all good bike shops.

As for rain, it falls in Britain in short bursts, with long dry periods. Only the optimistic and foolish ride in these conditions without mudguards and waterproofs. All bikes should have mudguards, but respectable factories have taken to fitting what, mysteriously, are called 'racing mudguards' – in other words, mudguards barely a foot long. When bikes were fragile and roads were poor, racing cyclists used these not to keep themselves dry but to stop muddy water jamming the brakes. Either the roads or the brakes improved because they fell out of fashion in the 1920s. Why, 60 years later, some people still fit them is a mystery. Throw them away.

Full-length mudguards – I recommend plastic ones – fit to the brake-fixing nuts (remember to re-tighten them!) and via stays to threaded eyelets brazed to the frame close to the wheel nuts. The stays hold the guards in place with a nut and bolt drilled to take the stay. It takes ten seconds to *think* you know how the nut, bolt and stay fit together, another ten seconds to take them to bits again, and a further ten seconds to get it right. The most prominent makers are Bluemel Brothers, at Wolston, Coventry CV8 3FU, but imported versions are available from makers such as Esge (distributed by R. J. Chicken and Sons, Bisley Works, Landpark Lane, Kensworth, Dunstable LU6 2PP), who boast that their guards can't be twisted permanently out of shape.

When you buy your mudguards, look for front guards that have two rather than one stay on each side. It's unlikely that it'll ever happen to you, but if for any reason something gets jammed between the tyre and the plastic, a mudguard with single stays just *might* crumple up and jam the front wheel, with unwelcome results.

If you're riding in the rain, raincoats are no good because they come open at the legs. Quilted anoraks are good but they soak through and let your legs get wet; nylon anoraks make you sweat like an old cheese. Traditionally, real cyclists have used billowing yellow or orange capes. They're not perfect – they swirl in a wind and they get clammy inside – but they're better than an anorak, quilted, nylon or otherwise. They also keep at least the top of your legs dry. Actually, if you wear shorts, wet legs dry quickly. Avoid wearing jeans, which get cold and wet in the rain and take ages to dry.

Cape manufacturers include: Bowden Weather Wear, of 39 Boswell Road, Sutton Coldfield B74 2NQ; Lillywhite-Lewis, of St John's House, Church Street, Princes Risborough, Bucks; and R. F. Developments, of St Neots, Cambs.

Always buy the biggest cape you can. You need one you can sit on to stop it blowing up your back and which is long enough at the front to hold with your thumbs. Buy a yellow one for first choice, never a dark one. And never buy one

Into every life . . . Traditional rain gear has for many years been the big yellow or orange cape. Slowly, it is being replaced by the neater but hugely more expensive Gore-Tex suit.
(Freestyle Sports)

of those jacket-sized 'racing' capes. They're fine if you're out training for racing, but otherwise they're useless. If they're waterproof, you'll drip with sweat; if they're semi-waterproof to dry up the sweat, they'll let the rain in.

If you've got a lot of money, you can buy waterproof suits made of a material like Gore-Tex, which is said to let in the air (for ventilation) but not the raindrops. They're pricey and reports vary. Gore-Tex is made by W. L. Gore and Associates, of Kirkton Campus, Livingston EH54 7BH (0506–412525). Gore-Tex suits are available from, among others: Berghaus, 34 Dean Street, Newcastle Upon Tyne NE1 1PG (091–232 3561); Ron Kitching, Hookstone Park, Harrogate, Yorkshire (0423–889077); Freewheel, 275 West End Lane, London NW6 1QS (01–450 0768); Bertram Dudley and Son, Commercial House, 1 Foundry Terrace, Bradford Road, Cleckheaton, Yorkshire.

BE POSITIVE

Be positive in everything you do – more positive than a car driver needs to be – and you'll hold your position on the road safely and surely. You ride on the left not to hide from faster traffic and avoid hindering it but because everyone travels on the left. So don't ride in the gutter. Take a positive position three or four feet out and hold it. There's no more an obligation on you to squeeze yourself into the kerb to let other road-users pass than there is for a motorist. Use friendly common sense.

Don't be arrogant, but remember that you belong on the road. Move out in time to complete a manoeuvre. Look for obstacles and start moving out 100 yards or more before them; the more consistent your speed and the more predictable your direction, the safer you will be. The worst you can do is ride up to a parked car and switch round it.

To move out in fast traffic, or on a narrow road, look back with plenty of time. Pick a spot in the traffic, stare the driver in the eye, stick out your arm, pick up speed, look him in the eye again and point down firmly at the space you intend to occupy. 'I'm moving out,' you're saying, 'and that's the space I'm moving into.' Move out straight away and give a wave of friendly acknowledgement. Be confident in your place on the road and others will respect that confidence.

3. Going for the Yellow

Cycling is for country lanes. There are miles of them, and when you divide cyclists into the length of lanes, and then remember that most drivers stick to main roads, you understand why people keep saying 'Don't see cyclists the way you did, do you?'

Not that lanes are perfect. You can be winging to the scent of summer flowers and mellowed hay when a roar will announce the arrival of a Used Bargain labelled 'Wayne and Tracy'. But at least lanes are better.

THE ROAD SYSTEM

At home, I've got a Girl Guide manual with useful hints on braille, semaphore, coating matches in wax, and mending punctures (using a bowl of water). The Advice for Cyclists section includes a warning that 'arterial routes' were to be renumbered. The Great North Road would become the A1, the Dover road the A2, the A3 would run to Portsmouth, the A4 to Bath, the A5 to Holyhead and the A6 to Manchester. The A7, A8 and A9 would all be in Scotland. From this point all the lesser roads would be numbered. And so you'll see that even today they follow the loose principle that roads starting between the A1 and the A2 will begin with a 1, those between the A2 and A3 with a 2, and so on.

Once the main roads were distinguished, lesser through routes took numbers starting with a B, and then purely local country lanes and busier town roads would take the letter C. These C roads would also have a number, but the number could be repeated in different districts and wouldn't generally be used. In fact, the only place I can think of where the signposts occasionally give the numbers is the Spalding area of south Lincolnshire.

In Ireland, they have a comparable system in which the main roads are either N or T (they're changing over) and local roads are L. Northern Ireland and the Isle of Man follow the British system but use the numbers over again.

Now, since motorists stick to the M (motorway) and A roads, you, as a cyclist, have got the Bs and the Cs. You won't be alone, of course – B roads in Sussex are busier than A roads in less populated counties like Northumberland. But the only time it's worth using A roads deliberately is when there's no alternative – a river crossing, perhaps; when the route is so picturesque it would be silly to do otherwise – like the North Devon coast road; or when you're just

And at the same time, the traffic was nose to tail on the M25.

in so much of a hurry that you want the straighter route and the smoother road surface. One more point comes to mind: A roads superseded by a motorway, like parts of the A4, are now a reasonably tranquil ride.

The law on riding these roads in company changes, it seems, with each edition of the Highway Code. The situation in 1989 was that you can ride two abreast except on narrow roads. Until then, the rule specified 'busy *and* narrow', which at least had a certain logic. As it stood after the alteration, though, it was permissible to ride two abreast on roads of near motorway speed and width, like the A1, but not on country lanes where, for such few cars as there are, you wouldn't hesitate to single out. Still, that's the law.

A GOOD MAP

Country lanes twist and turn and have surprise corners and sometimes misleading signposting. What you need is a good map.

Petrol station maps aren't much use because the scale's too small and there's no indication of height. They also concentrate and give too much precedence to main roads, because that's what most drivers want.

For many years cyclists in Britain chose the series produced by John Bartholomew in Edinburgh. It covered the country in 62 sheets, each of them about 60 miles by 40. Gradients weren't shown, but heights were, by different shades, varying from dark green through densities of brown to an ominous slate grey.

In its early years, the half-inch to the mile series was kept up-to-date by members of the CTC and many sections had map revision officers who'd write to 'Barts' and point out either where they'd got it wrong or where things had changed. This help was acknowledged on the maps.

Things went well until Barts followed the trend towards metrification. They published maps on paper or cloth, each a curious and attractive combination of the hand-drawn and the machine-printed, and they were good value for money. But with metrification to 1:100,000, or one centimetre to a kilometre, Barts

The law on riding two abreast is complicated, not least because the Highway Code keeps changing. But it's certainly not illegal and in quiet areas you can ride sociably for miles without disturbance.

made the mistake of enlarging the map photographically and, at the same time, removing some of the detail.

This had two sad effects. The first was that such errors as there were – usually generalizations of where roads went in built-up areas – became rather more obvious. You could read and forgive an old-style Barts map like a good friend, but the faults of personality became too blatant when they were enlarged. Second, some of the details omitted in the re-print were not only those that gave the new editions a 'thin' look, but also among the very things that cyclists most wanted.

The National, post-metrification, series had its adherents, but more and more cyclists switched instead to the by then much-improved Ordnance Survey alternative. The Ordnance Survey enlarged their maps photographically when they moved from an inch to a mile (1:63360) to the slightly larger two centimetres to the kilometre (1:50,000). They also, incidentally, maintained the original sheet size so that you got rather less map for your money. But the enlargement was only an interim stage. It was followed within a few years by a second edition reckoned by many to be the best blend of clarity, personality and accuracy that any cartographer had achieved.

The contour system – the pale brown lines linking points of equal height – had also been sorted out from the haphazard translation of the old feet and inches to something more worthwhile. It takes experience to read contour lines and, without the numbers, figure out whether you'll be going uphill or down. But it certainly takes no time at all to realize that the closer the contours are, the steeper the hill.

And so it's the OS map that I recommend, in the Landranger series, the ones with the garish magenta covers. It takes 204 sheets to cover Britain, each sheet covering 40 kilometres by 40 kilometres, or roughly 25 miles by 25 miles. That's not perfect, especially if you live on the corner of several maps, and you might have to take two or three maps with you for a full day's ride. For several days' rides you need correspondingly more maps. It also costs around £500 to buy the full set.

The 1:100,000 Barts maps in their red and black covers are still around, and at ⅝-inch to the mile they are the perfect scale for cycling. But the only place you're likely to find them now is in the kind of shop that sells remaindered books at cut price. They get more out of date as the years pass, but if you're prepared to come up against unexpected motorways and bypasses, they'll last you for many years yet.

Both Bartholomew and the Ordnance Survey, by the way, publish maps at smaller scales – around five miles to the inch, for example – but always at the cost of being harder to read, especially on the move, and a reduction of detail.

Now that the Barts Nationals have more or less gone, the largest scale the firm offers is the GT series, at 1:250,000. That's big enough to read and shows the A and B roads and many of the lanes; there are intermediate mileages along the bigger roads. But although they're good for planning – it takes only ten

Only a good map helps you find your way through forest paths like this. The Ordnance Survey comes to the rescue.

sheets to cover all England, Scotland and Wales – and for place-to-place riding where the intention is not to wander about too much, they're less than perfect for exploration on the spot.

The Ordnance Survey equivalent is the Routemaster series, at two centimetres to five kilometres, or about an inch to four miles. It has much the same information as the GT maps, perhaps better displayed. But it's printed on both sides of the paper, which can be as infuriating outdoors in the wind and rain as it is convenient indoors in the warm.

Unfortunately, with the exception of the few Ordnance Survey 'Tourist' maps, there's nothing in between that also shows heights and gradients. The Tourist series, still published at a mile to an inch, have not only the advantage of the more compact size but also of colour shading which gives an almost three-dimensional picture of hills. Therefore, as you'd guess, they're published only for hilly or even mountainous regions, namely the Cotswolds, Exmoor, Dartmoor, New Forest, Peak District, North York Moors, Loch Lomond, Trossachs, Ben Nevis and Glencoe. The Norfolk Broads, which are rather flatter, has an edition of its own at 1:50,000.

Using your map . . . and your head

You can follow signposts, but beware – signposts aren't put up with cyclists in mind. Sometimes traffic managers want cars and trucks away from certain villages, so they'll direct them from smaller to larger roads. As you approach a town, the signs point 90 degrees to the way you're going. You're following the direct lanes route, the signs beckon you to the main road.

It might not be just the peace of minor roads that tempts you to ignore the signs. You might want to avoid a climb. Remember that it's more comfortable to go *up* short, sharp climbs (contours placed closely together) and *down* long drags. This isn't the obvious way, but a few rides will show you that I'm right, especially into a headwind.

A chevron (>) across the road means a hill of between 1-in-7 and 1-in-5 (between 14 and 20 per cent, if you're getting used to the Continental system) and two chevrons (>>) mean steeper than 1-in-5, which is steep indeed. The chevrons always point downhill on OS maps, but they're shown only on coloured roads. On white roads and bridleways, you're left to read the contours.

One-in-five really is tough, even to walk – the kind of hill common only in Devon and Cornwall. They're tiring even on the descent. But it's best to be forewarned, so I offer this advice from *The Art and Pastime of Cycling* by R. J. Mercredy and A. J. Wilson, published in the last quarter of the 19th century:

> 'A day may come when your machine seems to get beyond your control, and fairly run away with you. In such a case, if you see that the hill is not very steep, and the bottom is in view . . . then stick to your saddle, keep cool and steer a straight course . . .
>
> 'If however, you wait too long [to dismount], and the machine is running at, say, 16 or 18 miles an hour, and going quicker each moment . . . you must not, no matter what the cost, stick to the saddle . . .
>
> 'If you find you are unable to dismount owing to the pace and steepness of the gradient, go for the nearest hedge or hawthorn bush and, just as you approach, throw your legs over the handles. You are sure to be hurt, but you may escape with only a few scrapes and bruises, whereas to hold on means more or less injury. If no hedge or hawthorn bush is near, throw your legs over the handles and put the brake hard on, and you will shoot forward and alight on your feet, when you must make every effort to keep on your feet and run as hard as you can, for your bicycle is in eager pursuit, and a stroke from it may place you *hors de combat*.'

Maps on the move

Reading a map attentively, so that you know not only where you are but what you can expect to see, means looking at it every mile. So if the lanes and junctions come too quickly, fix the map to the handlebars.

There are several ways to do this, including using a handlebar bag with a clear polythene pocket on top. Bags made on the Continent, though – and a lot of cycling equipment is made abroad, although the best bags come from Britain – have pockets designed for Michelin maps. Your OS won't fit without folding, and you might even have to trim the surplus off the cover.

The best solution is a map clip. The old-fashioned Plescher is a thin platform of alloy, about eight inches long, with two springs curving from the front to clamp the map. The other end fits to the nut of the handlebar stem. I don't think even the distributors (A. E. Griffiths, of Airport View, Coventry Road, Elmdon, Birmingham B26 3QS) would call them beautiful, but they work well. The problem is that they're inconvenient to remove and they fit only the now old-fashioned handlebar stems with fixing nuts. They were doomed when allen key fittings arrived.

The modern alternative is a clear plastic platform about four inches wide and five inches deep, taken back on itself so that the map can be wedged in place. The map is secure but it can wear quickly because it's a force fit. The platform fits the handlebars by two spring clips and the stem extension by a third clip. A lot of bike shops don't stock them, but they're available from the CTC shop at Godalming. You can (should) put the map in a plastic bag, trying not to tear the bag as you push it into the clip.

Never ever do more than glance at a map while you're moving – frequent fast glimpses will keep you well in the picture – and don't do even that in traffic or when there are other dangers close at hand.

Handlebar map carriers are difficult in the rain if you wear a big cape, because the plastic will cover the map. Even so, they're easier than repeatedly having to drag the map from your pocket and staring at it in the rain, getting it soaked and ruined.

Map references

Dorset council have an attractive habit of placing a circle on top of direction signs, with the OS grid reference on the rim, a blessing if you lose track of where you are.

To read a grid reference, open the map to show the numbers printed along the top and side margins. Pick the numbered line running to the left of the point you want to specify – 59, perhaps. That means the next to the right would be number 60. Place your point in tenths between the two lines; 59.6. Now repeat the process from the line below, again estimating the tenths above the line; say 08.2. Place the two figures together, remove the decimal points, and the six-digit figure is your grid reference: 596082. Working out where you are from the grid reference is the same procedure reversed.

Where to get your maps

Most booksellers, of course, sell maps. The range might be purely local, it might be global. It depends on the shop.

The Ordnance Survey itself is at Romsey Road, Maybush, Southampton SO9 4DH and has become markedly more commercial (and high-priced) since it became obliged to operate at a profit. The main agent for Scotland is Thomas Nelson and Sons, of 18 Dalkeith Road, Edinburgh EH16 5BS, and the main agent for England and Wales is Cook, Hammond and Kell, of 22–24 Caxton Street, London SW1H 0QU.

The Irish Ordnance Survey is at Phoenix Park, Dublin, and publishes maps at ½-inch to the mile (1:126,720) for the whole country and one inch to the mile for Cork, Dublin, Killarney and Wicklow. The Survey for Northern Ireland, at Upper Malone Road, Belfast BT9 5LA, covers the whole province at 1:50,000.

John Bartholomew and Son are at Duncan Street, Edinburgh EH9 1TA.

The biggest map retailers are:

CAMBRIDGE:	Heffer's Map Shop, 3 Green Street/Sidney Street, Cambridge (0223–350701).
EDINBURGH:	Bauermeister Booksellers, 19 George IV Bridge, Edinburgh EH1 1EH (031–226 5561).
LONDON:	McCarta, 122 King's Cross Road, London WC1X 9DS (01–278 8278).
	Stanford's International Map Centre, 12–14 Long Acre, Covent Garden, London WC2E 9LP (01–836 1321).
MANCHESTER:	W. H. Willshaw, 16 John Dalton Street, Manchester M2 6HS (061–834 0257).
OXFORD:	Blackwells, 50 Broad Street, Oxford (0865–792792).
WORCESTERSHIRE:	The Map Shop, A T. Atkinson and Partner, 15 High Street, Upton-upon-Severn, Worcs WR8 0JA (06846–3146).

From most or all of these you can buy that rare item, the unfolded map. This has two advantages. First, it costs less. And second, you can fold the map to the shape that suits you best. This is more important than it sounds at first, as you'll realize the first time you struggle with a map in a gale. Most riders don't bother, and just buy the pre-folded editions with their printed covers, but it's worth remembering that the option is open to you.

4. 'A Bloomin' Dook' or Country Riding

'The freshness of the dew was in the air; dew or the relics of an overnight shower glittered on the leaves and glass. Hoopdriver had breakfasted early by Mrs Gun's complaisance. He wheeled his machine up Putney Hill, and his heart sang within him. Halfway up, a dissipated black cat rushed home across the road and vanished under a gate. All the big red-brick houses behind the variegated shrubs and trees had their blinds down still, and he would not have changed places with a soul in any one of them for a hundred pounds . . .

'Hoopdriver mounted and, with a dignified curvature of path, began his great Cycling Tour along the Southern Coast.'

That was H. G. Wells's hero, the draper's assistant, liberated by two wheels in *Wheels of Chance*. It's one of three images I constantly conjure up. This is the first, with Hoopdriver whizzing down the other side of the hill – it was cycling after all which gave the world that delightful expression 'freewheeling' – and twanging his bell in sheer happiness.

' "He's a bloomin' dook – he is!" said Mr Hoopdriver to himself in a soft undertone, as he went soaring down the hill, and again: "He's a bloomin' dook!" He opened his mouth in a silent laugh . . .'

The second image is of an ink drawing by Frank Patterson. It shows one of his fresh-cheeked optimists pedalling in oilskins through a downpour. He's looking towards the artist with a faint, wry smile. The caption says: 'Better than mugging in an office, anyway'.

The third image, which balances the other two, is a cartoon by Johnny Helms. It shows a shattered cyclist who has ten or 20 miles still to go – miles that, for all his love of cycling, he wishes he didn't have to ride. An estate agent's board stands by the house that he's passing. 'For sale', it says, with the smaller inscription, 'If you lived here, you'd be home by now'.

There are satisfactions in riding huge distances day after day, and riders like Steve Gill of Liverpool advertise the fact commercially. But mile-eating isn't holiday-making, and it's hours of enjoyment that count and not miles. How far is up to you. There was a run of magazine correspondence recently about whether cycling clubs should cope with riders who wanted to cycle only 20 miles a day – or, more to the point, who *could* ride only 20 miles a day. Some thought they should, but one correspondent answered that anyone who wanted to cover only 20 miles in all the daylight hours that were available would be better off joining the Ramblers' Association.

Alan Leng, ex-director of the CTC, says most people would be astonished at how far they could ride if they wanted. Most could cover 40 miles or more in gentle countryside, he said. 'After all,' he reasoned, 'it's actually quite difficult to ride a bicycle at less than eight mph. You tend to fall off. So if you're out from nine until six, you can ride 40 miles in five hours and still have almost as long again to spend having lunch, cups of tea, or dangling your feet in a stream.'

You might not want to ride all day. There's no reason why you should. Thousands of people every summer pack their bikes in a caravan, spend a few hours pottering around the lanes and then pass the rest of the day sleeping, eating and drinking. Distance isn't important, but you might as well be aware of what you could do. Try 25 miles in a whole day, find somewhere for lunch and maybe an ancient home to look round, and you'll probably be home early as well as having a wonderful day. Next time you could go further.

RIGHTS OF WAY

Now that mountain bikes are getting popular, more and more folk are discovering that you don't have to stick to the road. More than that, they've cottoned on to the fact that cycling can often get even better if you don't.

The rather musty word for riding off-road is called rough-stuff, but it smacks a little of corduroy shorts and peaked caps. Mountain bike lovers (mountain bikes are simply high-quality sports bikes with tyres and clearances which cope with the mud) call it off-road riding and I can't think of a better description, since not all off-road riding is by any means rough.

To try it, though, and to cycle anywhere, you have to be aware of your rights of way. All coloured roads on an OS map are rights of way, but the white ones might not be. In fact, the law of trespass, despite those occasional signs saying: 'Trespassers Will Be Prosecuted', is lightweight. Even if you stray on to a private road by mistake, a smile and a few words can often secure a passage. If they don't – and a landowner may have good reasons for you not to ride through – you can be asked to leave by the quickest route, possibly back the way you came. Apologize pleasantly and do as you're asked.

Your rights off the road

Footpaths – The lowest form of right-of-way is a footpath. You have no particular right to be on one, and on some it would be a job to push let alone ride a bike anyway. On the other hand, most paths are lightly used and few people would object.

You wonder why it's best to stick to the yellow roads on your O.S. map? This, above Brecon in Wales, is the attraction.

Footpaths are among the oldest routes, linking long-forgotten settlements, or providing a route for farmworkers or for domestic staff working at the Big House. They were shown on seventh edition OS maps as a series of black dashes, but when rights of way were added, after completion of definitive maps, private paths were left in black and public routes changed to red. The exact symbol – and there's no alternative but to learn them – has changed in a couple of years. The Survey settled on red dashes just short enough to be mistaken for dots. The extent to which OS maps have been surveyed for rights of way is shown by a little pink map in the legend.

If you leave the path or strike off across private land, you could be sued for trespass. If you plough through crops, or panic animals, or leave gates open so that they stray, you could face a hefty claim for damages. In practice, in an empty field, the only damage would be bent blades of grass. Most farmers are country lovers. But remember that unless you're on a right of way, you've no more right to be there than the farmer has to be in your own back garden.

Years ago, a path had to be travelled a number of times a year to remain a right of way. Until the National Parks and Access to the Countryside Act in 1949, anyone who wanted to use a track had to prove that at some time the owner had dedicated it as a right of way. Ancient parish records had to be searched, and old people had to be found to show that walkers had used the

Bliss. Green lanes, like Mastiles Lane, give you that away-from-the-rest-of-the-world feeling. Bridleways can be pretty good as well, although rarely so wide.

path for as long as they could remember. A landowner could have a route closed because it hadn't been dedicated, and sometimes courts were eager to oblige. It took just a couple of magistrates, with the unfairness that there were more landowners among magistrates than in the population at large. A farmer could make sure his path wasn't used by letting it become unusable.

A sign reading 'Private' on a gateway can be both inaccurate and accurate. Land beyond the gate is private, but the path across it remains public. The owner might have put it up with that in mind, or he may have hoped that country-lovers would be confused and deterred. More bullying signs such as 'Beware fierce dogs' or 'Beware dangerous bull' rebound on the farmer; he has knowingly put people at risk on a right of way (although in some counties it's permissible to put 'safe' bulls in fields crossed by paths).

On this difficult subject, there is no precise law. Generally, no bull older than ten months is allowed untethered on its own in a field crossed by a public path. No bull of a recognized dairy breed (Ayrshire, British Friesian, British Holstein, Dairy Shorthorn, Guernsey, Jersey and Kerry) is ever allowed in a field crossed by a path. But beef and cross-bred bulls can be kept there provided there are also cows or heifers.

The Ramblers' Association (1–5 Wandsworth, London SW8 2XX) says: 'We believe that this is an ill-conceived law and no breed of bull can be relied upon to be entirely safe. We have several reports of so-called docile bulls becoming aggressive.'

Bridleways – Bridleways are wider and simpler to find. They're closer to being ordinary roads and farmers use them legally for tractors. Even so, the surface can vary dramatically. Clay can become impassable after rain; chalk remains firm but gets slippery.

Campaigning from the CTC led to cyclists having the right to use bridleways, on the basis that nobody could think of a good reason why they shouldn't. They're also used, as you might expect, by horse riders. Horse riders are on the whole pleasant and polite, in my experience, although occasionally sitting high on a magnificent animal can bring touches of arrogance. Probably the same can be said of cyclists. Either way, horses are nervous of cyclists and prone to swing towards them, leading with the tail. This is disconcerting for both cyclist and horseman, so for both your sakes, and because the law says you must, stop when you meet a horse on a bridleway.

Even on a wider pathway or road horses should be approached carefully. Coming from behind worries a horse most, since it hears a sound it can't recognize and then sees what it perceives to be a large whirring insect. Don't call out as you overtake; move as far across the road or the path as you can, or hesitate on a narrow pathway until the rider realizes you're there.

Advice in *The Art and Pastime of Cycling* still applies:

'Care should be taken by the cyclist not to startle any horse by passing at a high rate of speed, and upon meeting one which shows signs of restiveness he should ride slowly, and as far away as the width of the road permits, and should even stop if requested to do so by the driver.

'In most cases, though, it is better to proceed slowly and speak soothingly to the horse, as a sudden dismount when close at hand will startle more than anything else.

'The ground in front of a horse should not be taken until the rider is at least ten yards ahead. Horses standing by the roadside, unattended, should be approached with exceptional caution.'

Politeness and sense apply to walkers, too, individually or in groups. Nothing requires them to leap out of your way. They have a longer-rooted right to be there than you have! A polite 'Good morning' usually does the trick.

Bridleways are shown now on OS maps as red dashes.

RUPPs – Next up the scale is the 'road used as a public path', or RUPP. Town halls have been re-grading them as bridleways or by-ways. The difference is small. RUPPs and by-ways are considerable routes which have fallen into disuse. Some, like Mastiles Lane in the Dales, are five miles of delight.

By-ways are proper roads and, like any other road, open to all users. Because of the poor surface, the only cars on them are abandoned. But they *are* used by motorcyclists. The dispute about motorcyclists on public ways bubbles on. The more serious-minded riders belong to the Trail Riders Fellowship, a group of individuals who love the countryside and see no reason why they shouldn't explore it by motorcycle. Their machines are quiet and well-handled, and the riders preserve a good image.

Unfortunately, there are also motorcyclists who see by-ways as tracks for scrambling and trial riding. So often, their machines are insufficiently silenced. I was riding through the New Forest once, when the peace was shattered by long, nagging screams. I thought lumberjacks were felling trees somewhere, but truth dawned when three scramblers flew out of the undergrowth and off down the track. They were enjoying themselves; in the process they were spoiling beautiful countryside for me and anyone else who was enjoying it quietly.

Forest paths – Other tracks cross land belonging to the Forestry Commission. The Commission, like the National Trust, is a private landowner which has given walkers permission to cross but has stopped short of dedicating a right of way. Note that this applies only to walkers – cyclists have to ask permission. The Commission's information branch is at 231 Cortorphine Road, Edinburgh EH12 7NT, from where you can get a free leaflet, *See your Forests*, showing just where they are.

Why this distinction between walker and cyclist should have come about, I don't know. Many paths in Commission land stop when they reach particular plantations, but others are beautifully quiet connections between tranquil lanes.

*Unkind folk call them squirrel-squashers. Those who've tried a mountain bike know they're
ace on rough tracks. Note the straight, wide handlebars and the thick, knobbly tyres.*

Often they cut off stretches of main road, and the only other users are dog
walkers.

Scotland the brave

In Scotland it's all different. Cycling in Scotland is a mechanical aid to walking,
so that you're welcome on any route that can be used by walkers. Identifying
them on a map, though, is a different matter, because they're not shown as
rights of way. The chances are, though, that you won't be challenged on any

path outside the deer-stalking months of September and October, when they are shut to everyone.

The Scottish system reflects the fact that there's room for everyone who lives there. Much the same applies in Ireland, where nobody's ever thought it necessary to define rights of way and where you can ride where you like, although the landowner has the right to turf you off.

USEFUL CONTACTS

If you enjoy off-road riding, the *Mountain Bike Club* will put you in touch with fellow riders of mountain bikes. It has a newsletter, third party insurance, social events and races, on which it's quite keen. The address is Fanton House, Fanton Downham, Suffolk IP27 0TT (0842–812359).

The *Rough Stuff Fellowship* is a less rowdy organization, more concerned with seeing just how far from it all you can get with a bicycle. It's interested in off-road riding at all levels but engages in much conversation about difficult mountain passes with unpronounceable names. The address is 9 Liverpool Avenue, Southport PR8 3NE. It has a journal and a network of local clubs.

The Byways and Bridleways Trust is at 9 Queen Anne's Gate, London SW1H 9BY. The Countryside Commission, which is keen to open the countryside to everyone, cyclists or otherwise, is at John Dower House, Crescent Place, Cheltenham GL50 3RA; the Countryside Commission for Scotland is at Battleby, Redgorton, Perth PH1 3EW. The Open Spaces Society, whose name and enthusiasm is self-explanatory, is at 25a Bell Street, Henley-on-Thames, Oxfordshire RG9 2BA. Finally, the Scottish Rights of Way Society is at 28 Rutland Avenue, Edinburgh EH1 2BW.

5. The Good and the Bad

CLOTHING

You can make aches and pains from cycling less likely with suitable clothing.

In good weather, shorts are a blessing. Most shorts will do, although there's a trend towards specialized racing shorts. These come almost always in black, although the advent of triathlon riding has brought unbelievably colourful shorts on the scene, and they are usually longer in the leg than you might otherwise choose. They're extremely hard-wearing, they have no seams in the saddle area, and they're lined with chamois. The idea is that you wear them without underclothes and the chamois sticks to your skin, protecting you against abrasion from the saddle. In that way, the material can be made more thinly. The disadvantage is that they are skin tight, revealing every bulge of your body. If you can put up with that, and you don't mind the inflexibility of racing shorts when you climb off your bike (they're certainly less comfortable for walking round cathedrals and other tourist sights), then they're a good buy.

The other point is that neither the shorts nor your underwear should have prominent seams between you and the saddle. That's one of several reasons for not wearing jeans. Jeans are thin, too tight, too stiff (despite their thinness), too cold, absorb too much water and, as if that wasn't enough, they have tough seams where you least want them. If the weather's not good enough for shorts, try tracksuit bottoms.

Cycling tracksuits are tight in the leg, usually with ankle zips. They're higher at the back, to keep your back protected as you bend. If you don't bend forward much – if you have straight handlebars – you won't get much of a gap, but you might appreciate the extra protection that braces give you. Otherwise it's enough to wear a long jumper or jumpers.

Specialist tracksuit tops are also different. They have longer arms, again because of the odd position, and they're usually warmer, made of loop stitching so that you can ride into a cold breeze without freezing. In really cold weather, you'll be grateful for a ski hat and ski mitts, lined with fluffy wool and faced in nylon.

Oddly, the least suitable gear is cycle clips, which never hold your trousers the way you'd hope and because they're uncomfortably and unwisely tight. If you *have* to wear ordinary trousers, roll them up a couple of turns, which will look fine with white or no socks, and even better with brown legs. For dignity's sake, don't tuck your trousers into your socks!

SHOES

Your dead keen cyclists wear specialist cycling shoes, like running shoes without spikes. Instead, they have slotted shoe-plates or cleats to grip the pedal. The plates are great on the hills, but a nuisance when you get off and walk. My advice is that unless you want to ride 50 miles a day, or 20 miles at a time without stopping, conventional hard-soled trainers are fine, especially with soles ridged exactly crossways. The ridges will then slot on to metal pedals, although not, of course, on rubber pedals.

All lightweight dealers stock cycling shoes. Most are made on the Continent where, believe it or not, people have slightly thinner feet than the British. If that might be a problem, get in touch with Reynolds Cycles at Wellingborough Road, Northampton (0604–30586), which has been making cycling shoes to British widths for more than 40 years.

You can wear almost anything you like – even wellington boots, if you insist – on open pedals, but only lighter shoes like trainers if you've fitted toe-clips. By the way, don't wear running shoes with thick soles because you'll spend two-thirds of your energy on the pedals and the rest on compressing the sponge.

IN THE COLD

What else you wear depends on the weather, but remember that it can change fairly quickly and that it rains much more in the north and west than it does in the south and east. Remember, too, that August – which is high summer – is the second wettest month (after December).

Capes we've already looked at on page 18, but what do you do if (when) it turns bitterly cold? You could call it a day and leave your bike in the shed, of course. Or you could dress warmly and carry on riding.

The greatest problem is something called the wet-chill cycle. As you ride, however slowly, your temperature rises. And to compensate, you sweat a little. If you ride fast, you sweat more. In the summer that isn't really a problem because you're not wearing much and the free passage of air dries you.

With more clothing, of course, the air can't get at the damp patches. So, once you've stopped for a meal or a repair, and the sweat cools down, it takes a long time for your body to warm it up again. Some of the effort you wanted to devote to cycling, or merely maintaining body heat, has to be diverted to rewarming the chilled dampness.

Several thin layers are better than fewer thick ones; so are clever fabrics which draw perspiration through to the next layer. Helly Hansen, for example, make just such a vest. It stays dry, or dry-ish, while the T-shirt you wear on top gets damp. When you stop, the dampness seeps back slowly, but it takes a long time.

The long and lonely road. A bike, a back light, some waterproofs ... and you can go on for ever.

The other techniques are less scientific. You can wear thermal underwear – and never sneer at the value of long underpants – two pairs of thin socks, and lined and nylon-faced ski mitts. Specialist cycling tops with nylon fronts and jersey backs are also good value.

Finally, keep your head warm. A lot of body heat escapes through the scalp ... and even just around freezing, your ears will get as far as frost-nip if you don't protect them.

The countryside's not as attractive in winter, and daylight is shorter. But there's a beauty in the gaunt tracery of unleaved trees and the patterns of ridged snow in bare fields. Added to which, roads are emptier and tourist haunts almost neglected. Beware, though, the danger of wind chill. It rarely gets so cold in southern Britain that it's a risk, but the temperature still falls as you get faster. What is tolerable at walking pace approaches an arctic gale at 15 mph and a headwind.

WIND CHILL

Wind speed plus riding speed	Air temperature (°F)							
	50	40	30	20	10	0	−10	−20
5	48	37	27	16	6	−5	−15	−26
10	40	28	16	4	−9	−24	−33	−46
15	36	22	9	−5	−18	−32	−45	−58
20	32	18	4	−10	−25	−39	−53	−67
25	30	16	0	−15	−29	−44	−59	−74
30	28	13	−2	−18	−33	−48	−63	−79
35	27	11	−4	−20	−35	−51	−67	−82
40	26	10	−6	−21	−37	−53	−69	−85
	LITTLE DANGER			RISING DANGER				GREAT DANGER

If the worst does happen, take it seriously. The temperature doesn't have to fall far below freezing for your hands, ears, nose and toes to hurt and then start losing sensation. Don't rub the frozen parts or try to walk on frozen feet. Put frozen fingers under your armpits or in your groin. And then, as soon as you can, put the affected parts in water heated to body temperature. Then call a doctor.

HILLS AND HEADWINDS

Bikes are grand things for the flat, but not so good for hills. There is, in fact, an odd sort of satisfaction in cresting a long, hard hill. It's a great deal more fun than slogging into a headwind, anyway, which is never less than a soul-destroying business if you're not athletically fit.

Normally, as you ride, you use a little energy against the rolling resistance of the tyres, the hubs and all the other mechanical bits, and you use some to displace the air in front of you. At ten mph (16 kmh), the effort's shared equally. That assumes the road is flat and there's no wind. The faster you go in relation to the wind, the greater the energy you need. The effort of overcoming rolling resistance increases in direct proportion to the speed, but the effort for wind resistance is proportional to the cube of the combination of cycling speed and headwind speed.

Hol Crane, from the remarkable Crane family which includes the cousins

Nick and Dick (who rode deep into central China and up and down Mount Kilimanjaro), put the ratio like this:

MPH	6	10	15	20	22	24	26	28	30	32
Rolling resistance	6	10	15	20	22	24	26	28	30	32
Wind resistance	2	9	31	74	99	128	163	203	250	303

International Cycling Guide, 1980

This means, in turn, that you have to be careful what you do into a headwind. The more you fight it, the worse it'll get. Unless you're super-fit and you see every headwind as a challenge, the only sensible thing is to lower your speed and refuse to fight. It might take longer to get home – it *will* take longer to get home – but at least you'll get there.

Equally, it follows that the less resistance you offer to the wind, the less effort you'll need to overcome it. That's why racing bikes, which are made to be ridden as fast as possible, have dropped handlebars. You hold the lower rungs, you bend your back, and you hide from the wind. The best riders against the clock can hold a steady 30 mph with their backs parallel to the top tube.

Hills, of course, are commonly thought to be worse than a headwind but in fact are easier on three counts. First, wind resistance on a hill drops because your speed drops. Second, you can always get off and walk. And third, of course, a hill has to come to an end some time, whereas the headwind won't.

Again, even on a moderate drag – 1 in 27 – the energy you need rises wildly with the speed at which you tackle the climb:

MPH	6	10	15	20	22	24
Rolling resistance	6	10	15	20	22	24
Wind resistance	2	9	31	74	99	128
Energy for hill	40	67	100	133	147	160

International Cycling Guide, 1980

Since the least exhausting way to climb a hill is gently and evenly, that's the way to take it. At times, though, a hill can throw something much harder at you, like a tight corner or a slipped gear. And then you have to get out of the saddle and put all your weight directly on the pedals. The French call this riding '*en danseuse*', which actually makes it sound rather dainty. The English language, down-to-earth as ever, calls it 'honking'. Purists say you should never do it, but forget them. Sometimes it's the only way.

Honking is easiest with dropped handlebars because they're narrower and because the brake hoods point the right way for your hands. Nevertheless it's possible with flattish 'sports' bars, but impossible, just about, with sit-up-and-beg roadster bars. The trick is not just to stand on the pedals but to throw your weight further forwards and pull up on the right side of the handlebars as you push down on the right pedal. Then you pull the other side as you push the opposite pedal. It sounds moderately complicated. But you don't need to think of it after a few goes. It means you're using not only your leg power, but also your arms and shoulders and, of course, your sheer weight.

However, there's one further step you can take. I mentioned earlier that keen cyclists wear specialist shoes with metal or plastic, slotted plates fixed to the soles. By tightening the toestraps and locking your feet to the pedals, you can also pull up as well as push down, and drag the pedal round to the most difficult, upright position with the shoeplate.

Shoeplates and tight straps aren't for the nervous, though it *is* often possible to get your foot out of a tight pedal quickly, with a kind of sideways wrench – but not before your heart has skipped a beat.

STOPPING

The law – the Pedal Cycles (Construction and Use) Regulations 1983 – says you've got to have two brakes. If you ride a fixed wheel – one in which you can't stop the pedals turning – then that fixed wheel counts, legally, as a brake. That's because blokes with legs like tree trunks can stop the wheel going round just by stamping backwards on the pedals. My advice is to modify your bike to fit it with at least a freewheel, at best multiple gears, and to have two good brakes whether you've got a fixed wheel or not.

The front and back brake are not just copies of each other. It's the front brake that does the stopping, and the back brake that slows you or keeps the bike in a straight line as it stops. The old belief that you can jam on the front wheel and fly over the handlebars is a fallacy. At least, I've never known it happen. You can go flying – take a pearler, as they used to call it – if you hit something or something goes wrong, but not just by applying the brake.

In general, use the front brake if you want to stop or slow considerably, the back brake if you want just to check your progress, and both brakes if you have to stop suddenly. But beware: there are dangers in store for those who are not careful.

Whenever you use the front brake, the bike will decelerate quickly enough to move your weight forward. That puts more weight on the handlebars and, in turn, on the front tyre. The tyre has only so much adhesion, so you have to be cautious if you're on a greasy road or, worse, on leaves, slimy mud or gravel. The knack comes quickly but you still need to be aware all the time of the nature of road you're moving on to.

In principle, it's best to do as you would in a car – brake before the corner, while you're in a straight line, and let go as you start to take the corner. If you have to brake in the bend itself, perhaps because of a sudden obstruction, follow your instinct to pull the bike back upright against the gyroscopic effect of the wheels. This will happen anyway as you apply the brakes because it's only centrifugal force that keeps you stable as you're banked over. If the speed drops, you can't lean into the bend as much. And if you're upright, you can apply your brakes harder. This skill's called bike-handling and, like all skills, the only way you can learn is to do it a lot. Ride your bike whenever you can and it'll come instinctively.

Use both brakes intermittently if you want to check your speed on a long descent. Don't keep them on lightly all the time because the rims will heat up enough to start melting the glue on puncture patches – giving you another puncture.

And beware in the rain. Bike brakes don't behave consistently in the wet and dry. They're *much* worse in the wet and you need a lot of anticipation. Unfortunately, steel rims (the shiny, chromed ones) are spectacularly worse. It always strikes me as odd that you'd polish and smooth a braking surface. Add rainwater, of course, and it gets hideously slippery. Alloy rims aren't perfect, but they're infinitely better.

If you can, replace your steel rims with alloy ones. A bike shop will do the job for you and the wheels will spin better and make the bike lighter. And then, if you've got bog-standard brakes, ask the dealer to fit a good pair. You get more or less what you pay for. Fashion lends a hand at the very top end, but a good middle-priced brake will work wonders. Cheap ones are poorly made, work stiffly, use a lot of your hand pressure in operating the bearings, and are made of cheap mucky metal which is little better than sponge.

RIDING IN COMPANY

We've looked at what the law says about riding two-abreast. However determined you are to take your rights, the truth is that in many parts, especially in the south-east, it's no longer practical. Yet oddly, it becomes easier once there are four or more of you. You make a more solid body and, of course, your overall shape is more akin to a car or small van.

Four is a lovely number for a biking group. You ride in two pairs, the second pair just a couple of feet back from the pair in front. Since so much of cycling is overcoming air resistance and headwinds, the pair in front have a considerable slipstreaming effect. In time you won't even have to stare constantly at the back mudguards to make sure you are keeping your distance because it will come naturally.

Since they're doing more work than you are, rotate the lead every five miles or so. All you do is wait for a quiet stretch of road. Someone on the front shouts

'Changing!', the outside rider moves out a little, and the second pair rides through the gap in the middle. The leaders then slot on the back.

The other technique to perfect is singling out on narrow roads for overtaking traffic. This time the obligation is on the folk at the back to give the instruction. The outside front accelerates, the outside back decelerates, and everyone moves left. Hey presto – you're back in a straight line. Most drivers will be so impressed at the slickness and the courtesy that you'll get an acknowledging toot or wave, to which you should wave back. When it's safe, you double up again.

The thing to do is to keep together. You lose all the benefit if you break up. The only time gaps should open is on tough hills. Also, many riders, as they get out of the saddle to honk, inadvertently put their weight on both pedals rather than just the front one. For the person behind this is disastrous. The back wheel that was a polite 18 inches away now reverses alarmingly towards him! Shout a lot if this happens to you and the sinner may learn to repent and mend his ways.

6. Nights on the Road

There's only one thing better than going cycling for a day: going cycling for several days. It's a lovely experience to stay overnight and start again next morning on still fresher lanes.

WHERE TO STAY

Youth hostelling

The cheapest overnight accommodation is with friends or in your own caravan. But the other alternative is bed and breakfast at a youth hostel. They're run by national associations (one for England and Wales, one for Scotland, one for Northern Ireland, and one for the Republic). In Ireland there's also a loose federation of independent hostels, so it's best to join the national association. Membership is then valid all over the world.

You sleep in a bunk in a dormitory (a few hostels have family rooms), there may or may not be meals provided, and at most hostels you'll be asked to do a little work before you leave. The job's usually something mundane like sweeping the stairs, but I've been asked to groom a cat and tune the hostel piano. Several hostellers had tuned the piano before me, incidentally.

The YHA for England and Wales is at Trevelyan House, 8 St Stephen's Hill, St Albans, Hertfordshire AL1 2DY (0727–55215). The Scottish association is at 7 Glebe Crescent, Stirling FK8 2JA (0786–2821). The Northern Irish association is at 56 Bradbury Place, Belfast (0232–24733). The Irish association, An Oige, is at 39 Mountjoy Square, Dublin 1 (Dublin 745734). Between them they run about 400 hostels.

The word 'youth' is misleading. Hostels appeal to young people but in all except a few countries they're open to everyone over the age of 12. Hostellers younger than 12 have to be accompanied by adults. In Switzerland and Bavaria there's a maximum age of 27.

Sadly, membership of the YHA of England and Wales fell for many years and the hostels were forced to change their character and rules in order to attract greater numbers; they moved away from the original small, simple establishments with a strong communal flavour of the outdoors. There are now simple, standard, superior and special hostels, charging progressively higher prices. The buildings are still varied – a Norman castle on the Welsh border, an old

Tanners Hatch youth hostel in Surrey, a popular, simple hostel surrounded by woodlands on the Polesden Lacey estate. (Youth Hostels Association)

watermill in Winchester – but the occupants are less likely to be cyclists or genuine ramblers than hitch-hikers and school parties.

School parties cause most distress. The worst ones have not done enough to tire them in the day and teachers can't or won't keep control of them at night. The final straw for me came in Ireland where, feeling rather worse than Johnny Helms's 'you'd be home by now' hero, I and everyone else was kept awake until after 2 am by uncontrolled kids. I have never been hostelling again and I doubt that I ever will.

Peter Knottley, writing in *Cycling* as long ago as July 1967, said: 'I rode 85 miles to Inglesham youth hostel the other day – a slack time of year, midweek, and thus unbooked. This 20-bed hostel had 19 bookings, 17 of which consisted of a single school group. The warden had (I wonder why?) left the booking diary on the reception desk for all to see, and I duly saw and stole away.' He stayed instead in a bed and breakfast house, and so now do I.

Even so, I feel a pang of regret. Youth hostels *ought* to be better places. Sneakingly, I fear it's the onset of middle age in my case; hostels are still pretty popular with the under-20s.

Book at a hostel by sending the overnight fee for your age – the details are in the members' handbook – with a stamped addressed envelope. You can also now book the day before by telephone, but there's no central reservations service. Hostels in busy areas are full for much of the summer and booking is essential. But in most country hostels, you have a good chance of getting in on the off-chance, especially midweek or outside school holidays.

Another attractive youth hostel at Buxton in Derbyshire. (Youth Hostels Association)

Remember, though, that hostels usually close one night a week and some have restricted opening in the winter. They're also shut during much of the day, because the warden has other work to do. So it's pointless turning up at lunchtime and hoping for a bed for the night.

When you arrive, leave your bike in the shed and lock it. Walk to the entrance, report at the office, sign the book and hand in your membership card. If you haven't booked a meal, now's the time to ask. The warden might squeeze you in if you arrive close to 5 pm; evening meals are about 6.30 pm. Some hostels now have canteen or self-service meals. Otherwise you'll have to cook for yourself, usually in a large kitchen made to look small by enormous Australians. A hostel shop will have at least essential food – with bread sold by the slice, and milk, if it's available, by the cup or the pint.

The warden will also rent you a sheet sleeping bag if you don't own one. Pillows and blankets will be supplied. The hostel door is locked at night and lights-out, although it varies, is relatively early, to respect those who've been travelling all day. An early night is usually out of the question, though, because just when you are dropping off to sleep, so everyone else will come piling in at intervals, chattering away and turning on the lights. There's also a move towards hostels with juke boxes and television, but although the YHA insist that the sound won't carry to the dormitories, the old-guard aren't impressed.

You can cook your own breakfast or buy one from the hostel. Shrewd hostellers can then get away quickly because they'll have asked to do their job the previous evening. You can be away by 9 am, earlier if you cook your own breakfast, whereas the stair-sweepers and toilet-cleaners will be stranded until nearer 10 am. Collect your card, admire the stamp on the 'hostels visited' page, and pedal away.

Camping barns

As youth hostels move up market a little, something of the original flavour has returned with the introduction of camping barns. They're by no means national – there are only five and they've begun as an experiment. They provide little more than running water and a platform for your sleeping bag – which, along with your cooking arrangements, you bring for yourself.

They're open, as youth hostels were originally, only to cyclists and walkers. The place to inquire is Peak National Park Study Centre, Losehill Hall, Castleton, Derbyshire S30 2WB (0433–20373). The trend is likely to spread elsewhere and might, in time, become a national institution.

Bed and breakfast

The cost is a few pounds a night more than a youth hostel, for which you get precious little chance of meeting another cyclist but every chance of a good bed, a private room, hot showers and a good breakfast. You'll get fed up with each landlady in turn being astonished at how far you've ridden without distress, but that's a small penalty. Anyway, arriving by bike is usually good for extra pots of tea and breakfast.

Bed and breakfast places exist in abandon in Ireland and only a little less frequently in the more obvious parts of Britain. I'd take a chance any time in Ireland – even the smallest towns have a choice – but in Britain I always phone ahead at lunchtime. Over bank holidays, it's essential.

There are many bed and breakfast books, but the best is *Farm Holidays in Britain*, published by the Farm Holiday Bureau. Other books have more addresses but never the quality. There's little practical difference between a farmhouse and a town B and B, but farmhouses are in the country and often larger. The guide costs about £2, but the description 'in Britain' mysteriously excludes Scotland. Still, each entry has a small sketch of the house, a description, a guide to prices and, most useful, an Ordnance Survey grid reference. If you can't find the book locally, try the Farm Holiday Bureau at the National Agricultural Centre, Stoneleigh, near Kenilworth, Warwickshire CV8 2LZ.

District tourist boards keep lists of bed and breakfast houses and hotels for their own town and the surrounding countryside. They're shown by an 'i' sign on an OS map (1:50,000 scale), but not every office is open outside the main season. The bigger ones will make phone calls for you, to book a bed, either for a small fee or on commission. It's a useful service in tourist cities like Chester.

Alternatively, tourist offices will post their list to you, either for a phone call or the price of a stamped addressed envelope. Some – like Wiltshire and Norfolk – even have mapped cycle routes which, in Wiltshire, are signposted. You can get a list of all the tourist offices by asking for it, and it's well worth having.

The British Tourist Authority is at 64 St James's Street, London SW1 (01–629 9191). The English Tourist Board is at 4 Grosvenor Gardens, London SW1 (01–730 3400). The Wales Tourist Board is at Welcome House, High Street, Llandaff, Cardiff (0222–567701). The Isle of Man board is at 13 Victoria Street, Douglas (0624–4323). And the Scottish board is at 23 Ravelston Terrace, Edinburgh 4 (031–332 2433).

Additionally, the CTC produces a small list of bed and breakfast places in its handbook, price £1.75 to non-members. If you can't find a place on the approach to town, stop in the centre and ask for directions. Most towns have areas which specialize in small hotels and B and B establishments, usually because they've declined from the days when big houses were occupied by just one family. Most people are well aware where these areas are in their own town, so it's worth asking.

Not all landladies cook an evening meal, and those who do appreciate notice. If they don't cook, ask whether a local pub or café provides meals; you can then avoid an unwelcome ride in the dark in search of food.

Hotels

I've never stayed at anything but the smallest hotel on a cycling tour in Britain or Ireland, and only then because I couldn't find anywhere more modest. Prices start at the top end of the bed and breakfast range, although often with less comfort and fewer facilities. Hotels are commoner when cycling abroad, but we'll come to that in a moment. I suppose there are folk who stay at multi-starred hotels, but I don't think I'd enjoy their company on a bike tour.

Camping

The cheapest but most complicated accommodation is a tent. Camping has charms, but I don't recommend it if you haven't already been on a conventional bike tour. Not, that is, if you use a lightweight tent that can be moved every day. If you put up a bungalow tent and leave it in place, then the bike makes no difference.

Camping on wheels – bikepacking – can take you into the remotest places, but you need special equipment and you've got to accept the weight. It's fun but it's not 'soft' cycling. The holiday will be the cheapest and most independent you've had, but it takes several weeks away to recoup the cost of equipment.

Best of all is 'wild country' camping, away from established sites. It's easier in the west and north than the east, where more land is given over to crops. Most farmers will let you have a corner of a field if asked politely, and often for free.

In fact, it's frequently impossible to discover who owns odd corners of countryside and after a while you realize that no one's likely to object to a small tent going up for the night. If you've got more than one tent, you should always take trouble to find the landowner.

Campsites are convenient but noisier. You share them with large tents and caravans, but I always spend a night there every so often if only to get my washing done. There are no end of commercial guides to sites.

The Camping Club has its origins in the Association of Cycle Campers, the first form of organized camping, in 1901. Over the years the wheel has gone full circle and the Caravan Club has a section called the Association of Cycle and Lightweight Campers. There are five regional sections and a national magazine. You can get details from the Camping Club of Great Britain and Ireland at 11 Lower Grosvenor Place, London SW1W 0EY.

More about camping – equipment, and how to do it – in Chapter 7.

ORGANIZED HOLIDAYS

The YHA runs adventure holidays in Britain and abroad. The theme varies for each holiday and it might be purely for cycling or for cycling combined with

Clubs like the Cyclists' Touring Club give you a chance to get away for a day or longer with friends. Sadly, although the CTC is national, its individual sections can be widespread.

some other activity. Like those offered by the CTC, the holidays are led by enthusiasts whose only benefit is that their own costs are being covered.

The CTC's cycling holidays vary from beginners' tours to ambitious journeys across wild country in the Himalayas and Iceland. There are also private companies offering cycling holidays at home and abroad, particularly in France and Holland. Taking any of these trips is an ideal way to get into cycle touring, although naturally you've got to make sure that the trip you choose is graded to your ability.

In some cases, like CTC holidays, some trips get booked up soon after they're announced.

The advantages are that you have all the risks taken out for you, while preserving much of the adventure. You also have company, some of it hugely experienced, some of it at your own level. The disadvantage is that you lose the independence of a holiday alone or with just one or two companions.

In addition to the CTC and YHA, companies offering cycling holidays are listed below:

Anglo-Dutch Sports, 30a Foxgrove Road, Beckenham, Kent BR3 2BD (01–650 2347).
Bike Tours, PO Box 75, Bath BA1 1BX (0225–65786 or 310859).
Bottom Bracket Bike Tours, 13 Killerton Road, Bude, Cornwall EX23 8EL (0288–3618).
EACH Cycling Holidays, Holly Tree Farm, Yoxford, Suffolk IP17 3JP (072877–246).
Exmoor Mountain Bike Holidays, Warrs Farm Guest House, Luckwell Bridge, Wheddon Cross, near Minehead, Somerset (064384–263).
Four Seasons Cycling, The Old School House, St James Street, Castle Hedingham, Essex CO9 3EW (0787–61370).
Freewheeling Yorkshire, 16 Lawrence Street, York YO1 3BN (0904–20606).
Highland Cycle Tours, Aviemore, Invernesshire (0479–810729).
Joyrides, The Old Station, Machynlleth, Powys (0654–3109).
Just Pedalling, The Glass House, Wensum Street, Norwich NR3 1LA (0603–615200).
Peak National Park Study Centre, Losehill Hall, Castleton, Derbyshire S30 2WB (0433–20373 or 20693).
Scottish Cycling Holidays, Ballintuim Post Office, Blairgowie PH10 7NJ (025086–201).
Susi Madron's Cycling Holidays, 11 Norman Road, Platt Fields, Manchester M14 5LF (061–225 0739).
Tops Cycling Holidays, 43 Broad Street, Ross-on-Wye HR9 7DY (0989–64101).
Triskell Cycle Tours, 35 Langland Drive, Northway, Sedgley DY3 3TH (090783–78255).

Two Wheeler Tours, 8 Overbury Road, Parkstone, Dorset BH14 9JL (0202–741962).

Welsh Border Rides, 2 Pleasant View, Erwood, Builth Wells, Powys LD2 3EJ (09823–676).

The holidays that these companies offer vary a great deal. Some offer organized, led tours. Others do little more than provide basic information and book accommodation. Some are bigger and more active than others, others operate at home, others abroad, and some in many places. It's worth trying them all.

THE FIRST TIME

I recommend bed and breakfast for a first casual tour, with youth hostels as the alternative. Pick an easy route – avoiding the tightly-packed contours – and aim to cover 30 miles a day, always along the tiniest lanes and the better tracks. That way you can afford a few extra miles of diversion when something catches your attention. After all, touring is far from being just the amassing of miles; stop when you fancy and explore a village or admire a view. You'll know from your one-day rides how far you can manage on a longer trip – usually about ten or 15 miles less, because you'll be carrying luggage.

You might find it best to alternate 'long' and short days, using a half day's sightseeing around town to compensate for whatever aches and bruises you might have generated from unaccustomed cycling. You'll get the odd twinge, of course, if you haven't ridden much before. The most likely is a bruised backside. You'll wince when you get on the saddle on the second morning, but the good news is that the twinges go within a few miles. Actual soreness – redness or even abrasion of the skin – is not as common, but longer lasting. It's caused by clothing which rubs or by bare skin rubbing on the saddle. That's why cyclists wear longer shorts. Saddle pains disappear as you ride and finally go for good, but there's not much you can do about red skin except give it a break and change your clothing. Both afflictions are like punctures – less frequent than non-cyclists would have you believe.

Muscle aches are likely if you haven't ridden much before. There are hundreds of tiny arteries and veins running through your muscles and for some time they might not have expanded enough to let the sugared blood in and the waste products out. When that happens, acidity builds up in the muscles and the nerves translate it as an ache. There's nothing dangerous about it – it's a perfectly normal reaction – but the ache might remain until next morning if you haven't cleared the acidity as you sleep.

Actually, short of massage, the best way of reducing the acid is to go for another bike ride, but this time gently. Once you've arrived where you're staying, for example, get your bike out again after you've eaten and pootle round the village or perhaps to the pub for a small drink. The exercise will help reduce the morning's initial distress.

IN MY OLD KIT BAG

The first time I went touring, I stuffed everything in a duffel bag. I knew I'd made a mistake after the first ten miles. Never, ever, carry anything that weighs more than a camera on your shoulders. It'll shatter you, it'll make you wobble in crosswinds, and it'll make you miserable.

There's more good cycle luggage now than ever before. Traditionalists go for saddlebags made of black, canvas-like material and thick leather straps. They last for ever, mainly because the material wears only slightly and re-meshes whenever you scrape it against a wall. It's going out of fashion, though, superseded by nylon. Nylon bags are lighter, seal better (with a drawstring, which can't be fitted to the tougher canvas) and wear out faster. Scuff a nylon bag and the material won't re-mesh. Even so, they last many years.

Saddlebags are a British love and you can spot compatriots abroad as the ones with luggage hanging high over the back wheel. Continental tourists prefer handlebar bags, which are smaller, coupled with panniers hung over a rack

Never carry more than a camera on your back. Instead, spread the load round the bike – big bags at the back, smaller ones at the front. But remember that a loaded bike is heavier to steer as well as to pedal.

above the front wheel. You'll need panniers, anyway, if you're taking full camping gear, and some riders prefer them for any sort of tour because their centre of gravity is lower.

Handlebar bags are convenient but they make the steering feel heavy.

Least common are front panniers, probably because they need a fitment which is no use for anything else, because they make the steering heavy, and because the fitment takes some of the spring out of the forks. And there's always that feeling that front panniers are not quite big enough to be worth the trouble.

Whatever you buy, get the biggest size you can. Saddlebags, for example, are available with fold-back tops and extra, long straps. You can then use them for small or bulky loads. Remember to use the sidepockets for things you'll want on the road – maps, repair kit, light batteries and so on. And remember that, whatever the makers might prefer you to think, neither cotton nor nylon saddlebags or panniers are totally waterproof. Divide your kit into obvious groups and wrap them in plastic carrier bags. The day you don't do it is the day you wish you had. Put the kit into your bags in reverse order – the things you'll want last go in first. That way, even if you do have to open the bags in a storm, the most obvious things are on top.

For the same reason, roll your waterproofs into a convenient shape and fix them to the outside of your saddlebag. Never put capes *into* your luggage; it's inconvenient when they're dry, disastrous when they're wet.

Panniers range from the modest to tent-sized. The weight of the extra material is negligible and, although large bags cost more than small ones, it's still cheaper to buy one that's too big than two that are too small.

Where to buy bags

There are two main manufacturers in Britain and their bags are sold directly or by bike shops. Their addresses are: Carradice, Westmoreland Works, St Mary's Street, Nelson BE9 7BA (0282–65886), and Karrimor, Avenue Parade, Accrington, Lancs BB5 6PR.

There's also a growing range of imported bags, particularly from the United States.

Good bike baggage frames are made by Jim Blackburn and Esge and sold in most bike shops.

Kit lists

For a day or half-day ride I take:
    Cape
    Puncture repair kit and solution
    Tyre levers
    Spare jumper (in spring and autumn)
    Gloves (in winter and, occasionally, even summer)

For a weekend ride, staying in B and B, I take:
>   Everything above plus . . .
>   Washing gear
>   Trousers, shirt etc. for evening wear
>   Shoes and socks for evening wear
>   Spare underclothes
>   Spare rear brake cable (will also fit derailleur gear)
>   Chain rivet extractor
>   Spoke adjustment key
>   Small adjustable spanner
>   Two spare spokes

For a weekend ride, staying at youth hostels, I'd take:
>   Everything above plus . . .
>   Towel (provided at B and B)
>   Sheet sleeping bag
>   YHA membership card and handbook

For several days, I take:
>   Everything above plus . . .
>   Soap powder for washing out shirts and underwear
>   Small hair dryer (very useful for drying clothes!)
>   Spare shirts and socks
>   Lightweight nylon anorak for evening wear
>   Small screwdriver and the more essential allen keys

For a camping trip I take:
>   Everything above plus . . .
>   Tent
>   Sleeping bag
>   Cooking stove (once a paraffin Optimus but now a gas one)
>   Lightweight saucepans and frying pan
>   Plastic containers for food
>   Knife, fork and spoon
>   Tin opener
>   Washing-up gear
>   Light to use inside tent (although you're probably taking lights for the
>   bike)
>   Under-mat for sleeping bag
>   Cup
>   Fold-up water container
>   Matches

You might also like to add a book and a small radio if you're travelling alone for several days. I'm a radio fanatic. You'll certainly want to take money, cheque book and cards and all the other business of everyday life plus, I'm afraid, a padlock and chain.

You're then free to roam the British Isles . . .

Quiet lanes to far-away places . . .

7. Sleeping Under the Stars

What camping gives you, at best, is freedom. What it gives you, inevitably, is a big initial financial outlay and a lot of luggage. And what it gives you, occasionally, is rather less freedom. That last is a point which optimists overlook. Because in some parts of the country, you *can't* easily find either a campsite or a wild site.

But camping is still very worthwhile.

EQUIPMENT

Your tent

You'll scarcely recognize tents these days if your last experience was of Scout camping or holiday bungalow tents. They're lighter, tinier, harder-wearing and sometimes even quite different in shape. They're also misleadingly labelled, so that a two-man tent will accommodate two men who know each other quite well and a one-man tent is little more than a baggy pair of pyjamas.

The smaller the tent, the warmer it'll be. There's less room, it's true, but that's not so important if you'll be riding all day and sleeping all night. Provided you can store your gear and, if necessary, lean out of the tent to get a gas stove going in the outdoors (*never* in or very near the tent), that's all you need. Also, the smaller the tent, of course, the lighter it'll be and the easier to pack, both into its own bag and into your panniers. So, what do you look for?

First, there should be an inner tent with an outer tent that totally covers it. Don't buy a tent which has merely a flysheet, a kind of second roof, but on which the ends are left exposed, even if the latter are described as waterproof.

Second, it should have a sewn-in groundsheet which, when the tent is up, extends up the tent a few inches to stop insects and the like crawling in.

Third, it should have fully-extending zips in both the inner tent and the outer. Preferably the zips should operate from both ends and the entrances should line up.

Fourth, even if the tent slopes from front to back (many lightweight tents are smaller at the foot end than at the head), there should be room at each end to store things like muddy shoes, saddlebags and so on.

Fifth, the front entrance of the tent should be capable of being pegged out in such a way that you can shelter from the wind and rain but still have fresh air, and also so that you can prepare food in shelter.

Nothing beats wild camping for peace and relaxation, and a dark tent helps you blend in with the countryside.

Sixth, the poles should be telescopic.

Seventh, the guy ropes should be elasticated rather than 'string', and they should be short rather than long, if only because they're harder to trip over in the dark.

Eighth, the material of both inner and outer tent, but especially the outer tent, should be tear-resistant.

Ninth, the stress points, such as where the guy ropes join the tent, and the holes through which the poles protrude, should all be heavily reinforced.

Tenth, the edges should all be firmly finished off.

Tents were once universally ridge-shaped, as Baden-Powell would have recognized. Now they're not only no longer ridge-shaped, but they're no longer even particularly tent-shaped. You can get asymmetric ones, almost round ones, and wedge-shaped ones. The poles might be on the inside or outside; they might be upright or A-shaped. The range is endless.

Just about the only thing you can't have is a cotton tent. Most tents before the war were made of lightweight Egyptian cotton, but no longer. Now they're man-made fibres like nylon and terylene, although the makers usually give them fancier titles.

Fortunately, the people who sell tents – in specialized shops – generally know what they're talking about. But since you're buying something which will cost you a fair bit to start with and which you'll want to use for many years, it's worth looking around and going some way to find the right tent.

The CTC's York Rally is a good place to visit to help you make a decision. Hundreds of cyclists camp there each year. The point is that they've each chosen not just a lightweight tent, but one which particularly suits their individual needs. You can discuss these with them and narrow down your own choice. There are also occasional shows of lightweight tents, but it's never worth going to your ordinary local 'camping exhibition' because they're all bungalow tents and pop-up caravans.

Among the biggest tent suppliers are: Field and Trek, of 3 Wates Way, Brentwood, Essex CM15 9TB (0277-233122) and also in Canterbury, Kent.

Your sleeping bag

As with tents, it's worth paying as much as you can afford to get a really good sleeping bag – provided, of course, that you plan to go camping at all different times of year. If you only intend to camp in hot summer, then you don't need a bag that would keep you warm on a mountain in winter.

Bags are sold by seasons, so a three-season bag will get you through the spring, summer and autumn in theory, and a four-season bag should see you warm or even stifling at any time. There is some scientific backing to these claims, based on things called TOG values. But a little scepticism is called for. You won't necessarily be warm in a summer bag in mid-summer. It depends on how warm the tent is, whether you have an insulation mat beneath you (well recommended) and, of course, how warm the summer is. My own advice would be to get a three-season bag if only because in many summers there's not much distinction from early spring. And it has been known, in Britain, for snow to fall in June.

And here we come across another problem. Specialist sleeping bags are indeed made with cyclists and walkers in mind, both of whom have limited space for luggage. But the great majority of bags are made for the rest of the world, to whom a sleeping bag is just one more item to be thrown in the back of the car.

The best filling of all is real down, either goose or duck. It's warm, comfortable and light. It is, sadly, also rare and expensive. As a result, the 'down' bags you see on sale are actually a mixture of down and artificial fibre. The label will give you the proportions. At one time the exact mix was important. But now the artificial fillings are so much better that they're almost as good as the original down. They also hold water more briefly, whereas down gets matted as it dampens, and takes ages to dry.

The only drawback of artificial fillings is that they're bulkier. You'll get a cheaper sleeping bag but you'd be silly not to roll it up in the shop to see how simply it'll go in your touring bags. A bag made principally of down will roll up smaller than a pillow – say 20 × 30 centimetres.

Whatever the content, be sure that the bag's sewn into panels. If it's not, the filling will move about as you move about and eventually it'll all settle down at the bottom, leaving you mightily cold. And look closely at the stitching. It'll go right through from one side to the other on a cheap bag, because it doesn't cost as much to do it that way. It follows, though, that there's less and even no filling in and around the stitching, which means that's where the cold gets in. Better bags use a technique called slant pleating, which means more or less what it suggests – the stitching is angled in such a way that the bag isn't entirely closed; there's a raised edge, like the side of a box.

For the same reason, think twice about a bag with a zip, and never buy one with a full-length zip. Not only does the cold get in round the metal, but if there's no padding at the zip, the metal can get shockingly cold in the night and, maybe worse in the long run, the zip can jam irritatingly and even terminally on bits of grass, bramble and grit. It's not so bad if it jams shut, because you can still wriggle in as you would with an enclosed bag. It's disastrous if it jams open.

It's up to you whether you pick a bag with a padded hood. I've never felt the need for one, but then it's not often that I've gone camping in truly bitter weather. The little thin hood you *do* get on bags is intended not for your head but as a wrapper for the bag which will double as a pillowcase – into which you stuff rolled-up jumpers and anything else that's soft and not wanted overnight.

Many people also use cotton liners in their bags, of the sort that youth hostels insist on. They give a little extra warmth, and occasionally get all tangled up, but more importantly they keep the inside of the bag clean. You can't just go throwing a sleeping bag into a washing machine, not if it has got any natural filling. You have to buy soap made especially for sleeping bags and leave it to soak for hours in your bath. Then you hang it on the line and let it drip dry.

Since this takes a lot of time and can only be done when the weather's good, or at least dry, it follows that with the best will in the world you can't do it as often as you would choose. That's why you use the liner. They're thin, they're moderately easily washed and dried, even on tour (especially if you spend the occasional night on an organized site with a laundry room).

Finally, as I mentioned before, put something between you and the ground. The temperature in the tent will fall, but the air will stay warmer than outside because of your breathing and the heat that escapes through the bag. But the ground will stay cold and water in the earth will rise as the air temperature falls outside. In extreme conditions, it will freeze.

What you use is up to you. Even newspapers will help, if you have any. Personally, I use a garish yellow insulation mat, made of what looks like expanded polystyrene but is probably something rather more clever. It's very light, but it's also the most bulky bit of my kit. I carry it wrapped in plastic on top of the rack that supports the panniers.

An airbed might roll up smaller, but it's more than a hundred times heavier – far too heavy in my mind, and it also needs repumping every night. However, if you plan to stay in the same place all the time, you might not regard that as a handicap.

You can buy all these sorts of things from 'Camping and Outdoor' shops (which are actually run by the Scout Association and used to be called 'Scout' shops), from the various departments of Blacks, and from any other 'proper' camping shop. Places to avoid, as they are for anything more complicated and expensive than strips of puncture patches, are shops that sell mainly car bits and toys, and only cycling things on the side.

Your cooking gear

As a scout, I cooked on wood. Now I cook on gas. The choice you have, apart from wood, is methylated spirits, petrol, paraffin or bottled gas.

The cheapest is paraffin, but it's also tricky. Stoves like the Primus and the Optimus are moderately expensive to buy but last for ever if you look after them. They also churn out a massive amount of of heat. They demand a technique, though. For a start, you need a priming fuel in a small dish beneath the jet. You can use liquid or solid meths and you'll have to shelter it from the wind as it flickers and tries to warm up the jet so that the main fuel will vaporize.

If all goes well, you then pump up the pressure, the vaporized fuel rushes through the jet, you get a wonderful flame and the priming fuel burns itself out. If it goes wrong, though, you get a Red Adair oil blaze. The paraffin pours out of the jet neat and burns in a sooty yellow flame that won't go out in a hurry and clogs up the jet-hole, which you then have to prick clear.

Paraffin is easy to buy in Britain, but not always by the pint. The same applies to meths, of which you want only small quantities at a time. A paraffin stove, though, is extremely cheap to run.

Petrol stoves work in much the same way, but without so much fiddling about. The petrol is naturally much easier to buy but it's infinitely more dangerous than paraffin. If you thought the oil-well fire was spectacular with your paraffin stove, you should see what happens if you get it wrong with petrol. On the plus side, petrol stoves are inherently safer than their paraffin equivalent

A good tent is as small as you think you can manage and has a flysheet that you can peg open for ventilation with shelter . . . although cooking outdoors is even better on a lovely evening.

and only operator error makes them risky. The stove also packs down much smaller and into fewer pieces.

Methylated spirits stoves, like the Trangia, are making a comeback. For many years they weren't worth considering, but about ten years ago Trangia succeeded in making a lightweight combined stove and pan kit. Meths is reasonably simple to buy by the pint at hardware shops, but hardware shops don't abound in faraway areas. It's difficult to buy outside Britain. Operation is as simple as it's clean. You simply pour the spirit into a container and light it. It burns without smoke and for a reasonable time. The cost is higher than paraffin or petrol but not startlingly so.

The most convenient but also most expensive of all is bottled gas, of which Camping Gaz is the most prevalent. It's simple to light, produces good heat and is as safe as a naked flame can ever be. But there are drawbacks. For a start, you can only guess how much fuel you've got left, which means playing safe for much of the time and carrying a second canister. And second, it's not always possible to remove the canister from the stove attachment without the gas leaking out, which makes the whole thing more difficult to pack. A third disadvantage is that the gas canisters have to be carried in your bags, whereas petrol, paraffin and meths can be carried in a spare drinking bottle in a cage on the frame, which eases and spreads the load.

WHERE TO PITCH

There are no end of lists of organized campsites. Some are affiliated to the Camping Club, others are independent. Some are enormous and some are little more than a field behind a farmhouse. The smallest are delightful and almost – but not quite – as attractive as wild camping. They have, for example, running water and somewhere to wash. They're also reasonably secure, so that you can leave the tent with a calm mind and ride into the village to buy food. This is handy because food is both bulky and heavy, so the more you can buy and get through at each site, the less you've got to take with you next morning. Even so, you'll still end up carrying small quantities of sugar, tea and other bits and pieces, for which you'll want a variety of small plastic boxes and bags.

Wild camping is wonderful, so much so that it's worth almost any sort of inconvenience. And those inconveniences aren't always inconsiderable. You will get through quite a bit of water, for example, and it all has to be carried. If there's a house not too far away, you can take a folding plastic bucket and ask for a fill-up. But that might attract more attention than you would like.

High in the hills, where water runs over stone rather than through mud, the water is generally safe to drink provided it's tumbling fast and you've taken the precaution of walking half a mile or so up the river bank to make sure there are no dead sheep and no small boys relieving themselves. If you've got any doubts, use water purifying tablets and follow the instructions. I confess, in this country I've never used them. But then I've also mastered the art of using as little water as possible.

You have to start looking for your wild site early, say four o'clock in the afternoon. It can take a little time, riding gently all the while, looking away from the road towards the middle distance. You need a field, preferably with some trees, and no animals. Never pitch a tent where there are horses or, worse, cows. Cows are the dimmest of creatures and, whereas a horse will often sense that the tent is 'unsafe', a cow will be riddled with curiosity, which it expresses by walking over your accommodation. If you pitch in half-light, do look very closely. Cows and even sheep are pretty big things, but they lie down and hide away, and if you're tired, you might not see them.

Unfortunately, pasture or meadow land is what you need. You can't pitch where there are crops. And pasture land, in much of the country, is getting scarce. As you look, stop at a café or pub and slake your thirst. You'll be fairly dehydrated after a lot of riding, so drink now. You might also ask whether anybody knows of a decent pitch and who owns the land.

You should look for moderately level ground, well drained, sheltered by trees, with access to either tap or fresh running water, away from both roads and railway lines.

If there's no real wind, pitch with your head up the slope. If there's a strong wind, pitch on as level ground as possible but always with the tail of the tent, which in many cases is the lower end, into the gale.

When you looked at tents in the shop, you were probably offered a choice between dark green and a range of garish colours, principally orange. Now you'll see the advantage of dark green. An orange tent will stand out wherever you put it. Even if you're there entirely legitimately, as you would be on a campsite, the lurid, unnatural colour is offensive against the countryside. It's great up a snowy mountain while you're waiting for the rescue helicopter, but not in a meadow in Dorset. From this you'll gather that I have occasionally pitched without permission. If there is just one tent, if you genuinely can't trace the owner of the land, if there are neither animals nor crops, and you're there just for one night, I doubt that anybody would object. And in my case they never have.

Having satisfied my thirst, had a wash and made inquiries locally, I fill two one-pint drinking bottles with water and go pitch my tent. Those two pints will later cook my potatoes, make me a mug of tea in the evening and the following morning, and leave me enough for a fair if not wonderful wash. I can then stop at a café, pub or even toilet washroom the next day and complete the job.

The advantage of a little green tent – and my solo tent has to be entered like a sleeping bag, almost horizontally – is that it vanishes almost as soon as it goes up against a dark background. That means I feel fairly happy about leaving it to ride back into the village to buy food (for which I recommend carrying a couple of old-fashioned string shopping bags, which weigh nothing and which will save you unloading your bike bags).

How you store the bike overnight is up to you. On public campsites I always remove one wheel and lock it to the frame, then lock the whole thing round something immovable. Paranoia, perhaps, but if there's one thing calculated to spoil a cycling holiday it's the absence of a bike in the morning. If I can't lock it to anything, I lay my bike on the ground and loop one of the guy ropes through the frame. This is supposed to suggest that the slightest movement to the bike will wake its owner, who will emerge from the tent like an enraged bull. However, as anybody with half a gram of sense will realize, this is unlikely on almost every count!

Up and down

Finally, never go camping with a tent that you can't pitch in the dark. After all, it might happen. More to the point, if you can pitch it in the dark, you can also do it quickly in bad weather. I have two tents and the first one I bought in a hurry; it's a lovely tent, with plenty of room, but it's asymmetric and although the outer tent is easy to put up, it's impossible to decide which way the inner tent should go. Therefore your chances are never better than 50 per cent that you won't have to de-rig and start again.

On a lovely summer's afternoon, it doesn't much matter in which order you do things. But in the rain it does. If your tent allows it (a good point to check when you're buying) put up the waterproof outer tent first. The inner tent will then stay dry and you can fix it inside.

When you strike camp in the morning, leave the tent itself to last, and the outer tent to very last. Pack everything that will go into your bike bags, then take down the inner tent and put it into a bag of its own. Then, finally, take down the outer tent. Both inner and outer will be wet – the inner if only from condensation – but the outer will be wetter and grubbier. The outer tent won't rot but the inner will, so putting it in a separate bag means you can pull it out and part-dry it when the weather improves later in the day.

Finally, have a technique for collecting the tent pegs. Go round the tent in a set order and keep to that order every time. Don't throw pegs into a heap – carry them. One lost tent peg isn't a disaster . . . but every one after that certainly will be.

CAMPING CARNETS

Now's not the time to go in detail into the business of cycling abroad. But when you do, and you take your tent, you'll find yourself being asked for a thing called a camping carnet (pronounced car-nay).

It establishes that you're a bona-fide camper, whatever that might be, and more importantly that you have third-party insurance. You can get one from the CTC, the AA and the RAC without difficulty.

CHECKLIST OF THINGS TO TAKE

Tent	Sleeping bag
Insulation mat	Inner liner
Stove and fuel	Set of nesting pans (2)
Frying pan (or pan lid and handle)	Matches
Folding water bucket	Extra bike bottles
String shopping bag	Torch (or front light)

8. And the Kids Came Too

KIDDY CRANKS

The greatest fall-out from any time-consuming activity – and if nothing else, cycling is precisely that – comes with the birth of children. Having children is the greatest time-consuming activity of all. Some never return to whatever they were doing before. Some carry on regardless, and I've known women riding well into pregnancy and then again soon after childbirth.

The problem, of course, is that cycling is a mechanical exercise. Either a child has to pedal itself or it has to be pedalled. Whatever method you choose, when a child is involved, the penalty is a much slower, sometimes painfully slower, pace. Even so, it's far from impossible.

I remember running a cycle race once in a town called Berkhamsted, which is in north-west Hertfordshire. One of the spectators was a father who had ridden with his son, from Hatfield, about ten miles away. The son couldn't have been more than seven and was quite happy to spend the rest of the day cycling as well, if necessary. In fact, the son struck me as rather fitter than his father!

Young cyclists have problems of their own. Their limitations are stamina, which it would be unwise to challenge, and size, which is directly related to the kind of bike they can use. You could take a child cycling with stabilizers – those little wheels that sprout from the back hub – but it wouldn't be any more enjoyable for him than for you. Better to start as soon as you can with something approaching an adult bike. This means – and it's a sad fact if you're already committed – that fad bikes such as BMX racers, Choppers and the like are unsuitable.

When I was general secretary of the English Schools Cycling Association (6 Malmerswell Road, High Wycombe, Bucks HP13 6PD; telephone 0494–446857), I always felt that I ought to encourage kids who turned up on these peculiar bikes – bikes that were more the product of a marketing man's mind than a real cyclist's experience. Oh, I tried hard enough. But in the end all I could do was concede that for anything more advanced than obstacle races and cycling round the school running track, fancy bikes were a dead loss. They're usually highly mobile at low speeds and often designed for a degree of trick riding. But beyond that they're hopeless. They're also, to my distress, designed to resemble motorcycles.

Now, I'm not a Luddite. I'm not determined to stand in the way of progress. But bikes have been pretty standard for a great many years and the only brain to have produced something at least comparable yet different – and only then with a great many compromises – was Alex Moulton with his small-wheeler in the sixties.

The happy news is that, since children grow up, there's always a market in second-hand equipment. Some of the more specialized bikes are *only* available on the second-hand market, advertised in magazines like *Cycling Weekly* and, more especially, in the CTC's magazine, *Cycletouring*.

Really, as soon as children can hold themselves upright, they're ready to travel in kiddy-seats. You can't ride far, though, for two good reasons. First, young muscles tire quickly, and it's a tiring business sitting on one of those seats as the bike bumps its way down the road. Second, *you* can ride in almost any temperature because your effort keeps you warm. But nipper on the kiddy-seat is making no more effort than staying upright. And he's soon a victim to wind-chill – the phenomenon whereby temperature falls rapidly as the wind starts blowing. It may be warm for you, but it can be ten or fifteen degrees colder in the passenger seat. There is, anyway, the extra weight of carrying a child, so the process is probably self-limiting.

Your only practical choice is whether to carry fore or aft. Little padded seats on the top tube are non-starters. Front seats are restricted by space, so they suit only smaller children. They also make the steering insensitive. You can, though, talk to your passenger and keep an eye on him; the penalty is that he is exposed to the wind. Back seats fit to carriers over the wheel, and there are metal and plastic versions to choose from, each with guards to stop small legs going into the spokes. The back is warmer and a little drier. But if your passenger dozes and lolls sideways, you'll notice the effect on your balance.

And balance is critical, of course, because if the bike topples over your passenger could come off worse than you. Having a child in a seat, however, is by no means as dangerous as you might think. And balance includes not only while you're riding, which is probably the safest period, but while the bike is at a standstill. You have to be able to stop, dismount and remove your passenger without mishap.

Sally Barrett, who has two children, started cycling with them when they were three and 18 months. In *Cycletouring*, she said: 'We would recommend the high-back child seats, as they support the child asleep and a child of three can unbalance a bike if he falls to one side. Having said that, we have always managed with low-back, old-fashioned, black steel seats, since our eldest weighed 40 lb when we started and I still haven't heard of a modern seat taking more than 40 lb.

'Of course, we strap them in and they now wear crash helmets. It only needs a slight blow to the skull to kill or seriously maim – a couple of times my bike has overbalanced while stationary and if the child's head had met a kerb stone there would have been a serious accident. We put our children into canoe helmets as they are fully adaptable and we could not have afforded the five to seven bike helmets needed to fit their developing head sizes.'

I've never believed in the worth of cycling crash helmets, but in this case I agree. To be honest, carrying a young child in a seat on the back of a single or tandem seems too risky. It's not *that* long before children are old enough to start pedalling in their own right.

Trailers

An eccentric middle stage between a rear seat and a separate bike is a device called a Rann trailer or its successor, the Hann trailer (almost exactly the same but built by a Mr Hannington of Berkshire). Both look like children's bikes with their front wheels removed. The end of what would be the steering head fixes instead to a bearing behind the main bike. Where one goes, the other follows, but in this case pedalling as well. It takes no more than a few minutes to disconnect the trailer for a lone ride.

I'm not sure whether either Mr Rann or Mr Hann are still turning out their products – I rather hope so because of their wonderful, uniquely British eccentricity and practicability. But they certainly can't be producing them in vast quantities because you don't often see them in use. Like sidecars, they occasionally change hands through the advertisements in *Cycletouring* or through the private mafia of family cyclists who converge yearly on the CTC's York Rally. General-purpose bike trailers, which would also carry children, are made by Woodland World, Saffron Walden, Essex CB11 3BR (Freephone 3613).

A trailer by Mr Rann . . . or was it Mr Hann? It's articulated to make the corners easier.

Small bikes

Children's bikes follow the same rules as adult machines, but they give the frame-builder problems. Children have shorter cranks, so the bottom bracket can be nearer the ground, but there still has to be ground clearance on corners. Therefore it's often not possible to raise the saddle as high as it ought to be if the rider still has to reach the ground without getting off the saddle.

Well-intending policemen, who are more accustomed to road safety lectures than to cycling, are apt to advise youngsters to place one or both feet squarely on the ground while stationary. A moment's thought reveals that this is just about impossible if the bike is to be pedalled as well. Compromise is essential for safety, but children grow in spurts, so be prepared to put the saddle up frequently, a centimetre at a time, with at least a week between each increase. Remember that the saddle should never be raised leaving less than two inches of seat pin hidden in the tube.

Tim Hughes, one of the country's leading tourists, had a frame built for his first child just before his seventh birthday. The smallest that looked possible with 26-inch wheels was 18½ inches, and only then with a curved or sloping top tube to get the saddle low enough. Whether you go to that expense is up to you – I doubt that you'd want to – but the rule applies. If you *did* get something built specially, it may be fairly expensive but you could be sure of selling it afterwards. Even small adult frames sell better second-hand than large ones.

As Tim said: 'It was only the fact that it had about a dozen years of prospective usefulness for three children that made it, to us, an economic proposition.'

Obviously if 18½ is the smallest frame that will take full-sized wheels (there are three basic adult wheels – 27 and 26 inches, and 700 millimetres), smaller frames will take smaller wheels. There's no shortage of children's bikes in this area – 20-inch wheels are common – but take care that you can fit multiple gears if they're not already fitted (which, apart from possibly a three-speed hub gear, is unlikely). The dealer will advise you. Alternatively, frame-builders like Dave Russell at 16–18 Chalvey Road East, Slough, Berks, will make high-quality frames in small sizes.

Never change the size artificially – by fixing blocks to the pedals, for example, or even by fitting much shorter cranks. You might make the leg-length right but the effective bottom bracket height will rise, making it difficult to reach the ground, as well as making the bike uncomfortable. The same applies to reversing or upturning handlebars to shorten the reach.

The only acceptable ruse is to take a standard saddle clip (the part that connects the seat pin to the saddle frame) and reverse it. Saddle clips raise the saddle a little, so turning one upside down will lower it. There's only a small difference. Obviously, if the bike has a one-piece pin and clamp, there's nothing you can do except buy a new and, you'll be pleased to hear, cheaper one.

Whatever you do, never buy a low-quality children's bike in case your offspring don't take to cycling. Why commit a youngster to pushing around something sluggish and unappealing when you wouldn't be prepared to do the same? It *guarantees* that a youngster won't enjoy it. The difference in price is often less than you would think. Fashion bikes carry fancy prices, like all fashion goods. They also lose value quickly. Traditional children's bikes, well maintained, hold their value well.

Things to look for, apart from ball rather than sintered bearings, include:

– good, lively brakes with small but effective brake levers;
– plenty of scope to raise the saddle and handlebars;
– a traditional diamond or girls' type open frame (preferably a mixte frame for girls, in which there are parallel diagonal tubes);
– normal pneumatic tyres which take a good high pressure (preferably at least 60 psi);
– variable gears such as a Sturmey Archer hub gear or, for children over 11, possibly a derailleur gear.

Stick to a traditional design and an established manufacturer, such as Raleigh, Dawes, Falcon and Peugeot and you won't go far wrong. You can either re-sell as your child grows or maintain the bike and pass it down to younger offspring, which makes your outlay lower in the long run.

There's more information on buying bicycles in the next chapter.

By tandem

The other way to take young children is by tandem, adapting the backseat with extension pedals to shorten the leg-length. You may also have to extend the handlebars backwards. You can get kiddy-crank sets from Ken Rogers, at 71 Berkeley Avenue, Cranford, Hounslow, Middlesex TW4 6LF. This sounds an attractive proposition, and it's certainly homely. But before you get too enthusiastic, remember that it's hard to ride a tandem with no real push coming from the back. And tandems aren't cheap – say £500 for a low-quality one, rather more than twice as much for a lightweight.

Factories such as Peugeot now make moderately-priced tandems (sold through affiliated shops), although most as-supplied machines have standard frame sizes – say 22 inches front and back, which means that you have to be a pretty average size unless you want the saddle right up or right down. More than that, it means that two adults riding together have to be much the same size.

To have a frame built with less balanced sizes (in fact, to have a tandem frame of any size built specially) naturally costs rather more. The advantage, though, is that the child will grow to fit the tandem and that tandems always sell well second-hand. If your offspring tires on a ride, you can always get him home, even if you get more tired in the process. An exhausted child in a kiddy-seat, or worse, on his own machine, is no joke.

Kiddy-cranks . . . the extra chain and the raised pedals at the back make the tandem a possibility for growing children.

Among the specialists are Bob Jackson at 148 Harehills Lane, Leeds LS8 5BD (0532–622088); Mercian Cycles, at 7 Shardlow Road, Alvaston, Derby DE2 0JG (0332–752468); and the Tandem and Cycle Centre at 281 Old Kent Road, London SE1 (01–231 1641).

You can obtain more information from Mrs C. Blackman, the secretary of the Tandem Club, at 8 Newnham Road, Hook, Basingstoke, Hampshire RG27

9LX. The club's magazine is a wonderful source not only of advice and anecdote but also of spares.

Sidecars

A further option is to add something to either your single cycle or your tandem. There used to be things called Watsonian sidecars – other people may have made them as well, but they're the ones that stand out in my memory – like junior versions of motorcycle sidecars. You still see them advertised from time to time.

They sound impossibly hard work on a single bike – indeed, I've only ever *heard* of them on singles and never actually seen one – but parents who've had them on their tandem tell me they're practical. The snag with a tandem is that for all its nippiness on the flat, it's sluggish up hills. And adding a sidecar, I'm sure, will do nothing to improve things. It'll make you a lot stronger, though! A friend of mine in Essex pedalled her first child around in one for months and the effect, when she took it off to ride long-distance rallies, was phenomenal. She rode permanently in a gear a good 20 inches higher than anyone else.

Advertise in *Cycletouring* if you want one (contact Cecilia Clack, CTC, 69 Meadrow, Godalming, Surrey GU7 3HS; 04868–7217) or visit the York Rally on the Knavesmire in the summer for information (dates, again, from the CTC).

YOUNGSTERS ON THE ROAD

Doing your own pedalling isn't the same as being a scaled-down adult. Children have a higher centre of gravity – which is why toddlers fall over so often – and most don't reach an adult balance until around their fifteenth birthday. They're also less resistant to cold or fatigue, two points easy to overlook. Just because you, the adult, feel fresh, warm and fine, there's no reason to suppose that nipper will as well.

There's more than a purely physiological problem; youngsters can ride a surprising distance, as that kiddy in Berkhamsted proved. But boredom comes more quickly, producing tiredness faster. Children need constant stimulation, and their attention span is annoyingly brief. They also don't see any great inner joy in pedalling; cycling is often to them a way of getting to different places, and for many years it will be the places that are valued more highly than the riding. You'll need frequent stops – right down to every ten minutes for real youngsters – to investigate streams, look at squirrels, kick conkers or play in parks.

And remember that children aren't strong. Even hefty youngsters can put out a few hard efforts but tire quickly after repeated pedalling. Keep gears very low, which in turn means slow speeds and shortened distances. And concepts which to you seem obvious might be no such thing to a younger mind. For example, I was riding with a five-year-old on her first bike, carefully shepherding her on the quietest of lanes. The low gears and the small wheels stopped the bike running away on the gentle downhills, but the first incline produced both effort and puzzlement. The little girl, struggling for an explanation, complained in exasperation: 'My pedals are getting stiff . . .'

I was given my first bike when I was twelve, several years older than most of my friends, and I was kept off main roads until I was thirteen. And they were the main roads of 1960, not the mega-highways of today. I hate to think what it must be like to start cycling in the suburbs now, but I suppose we all adapt to circumstances, and perhaps children are no more terrified by today's roads than I was by the busiest highways of 1960. That doesn't mean that you can cast youngsters on the open road without a care. That would be foolish. But there are still quiet side roads on which to learn and, as I said earlier, it's a rare town that doesn't have some quiet escape from its centre.

Cycling round side roads developed my riding skill, and a sense of adventure and self-preservation taught me the rest. I took the RoSPA test at twelve, I think, and while I'm not sure it did me the slightest good (although it may have changed since then), I don't suppose it did me any harm. I would recommend it to anyone. Riding in traffic is a question of self-confidence and recognition that you're *part* of the traffic flow and not merely an adjunct to it. That's something that children take more for granted and, with guidance, this attitude ought to be encouraged.

By the age of fourteen, I was riding 40 miles a day with any mate who could keep up (and occasionally with friends with whom I couldn't keep up), and soon after my fifteenth birthday I joined a cycling club – the Edgware section of the CTC. Since then, cycling has taken me in one way or another over much of the world and certainly all over Britain. It is, as my mother would have pointed out despairingly, the only thing that her rapidly-bored son stuck at.

ADVENTURE FOR CHILDREN

There's a challenge for youngsters who really grow into cycling. The Duke of Edinburgh's award scheme, for example, includes cycling as one of its adventure options. The address for details of the award is: Duke of Edinburgh's Award Scheme, 5 Prince of Wales Terrace, Kensington, London W8.

The CTC offers a Touring Explorers' Award, not necessarily for children but for any newcomers to the sport. The idea is to explore one county and then, eventually the whole country, answering questions set by CTC headquarters. There are different grades of achievement, culminating in the Super Tourist Award. It's a wonderful way of interesting young riders and setting a competitive tone. Details can be obtained from CTC headquarters; remember to state which county interests you.

There is also for children the option of riding BMX – bicycle moto-cross.

The sport hasn't lived up to the initial boom of the late seventies, but it's very far from being moribund. It's certainly lively enough to have several magazines devoted to it, and more than one national organization. The addresses are: National BMX Association, Litho House, Heath Road, Ashton-in-Makerfield, Wigan WN4 9DY; UKBMX, Mrs S. Jarvis, 5 Church Hill, Staplehurst, Tonbridge, Kent TN12 0AY.

Remember, though, that BMX bikes are strictly competition machines and no more suited to general leisure riding than a featherweight Tour de France racer.

you'll be hanging around, possibly in the cold, certainly in the motor exhaust and bluster of the quayside.

You can buy tickets at any travel agent, from the ferry company itself or on the outskirts of Dover from a number of garages on the approach to the town. The price is the same wherever you pay. There is no need to book in advance, unless you're crossing from Hull, Newcastle or Plymouth. Ferries from those ports make much longer crossings and a booked cabin, or at least a booked reclining seat, is advisable or even compulsory.

You might like to know, by the way, that there are day return fares on routes between the south-east and Belgium and France. They're not generally advertised in the brochures but they can often be cheaper than the standard one-way fare.

On the ship, you'll be directed into a poky corner of the car deck. Should the area be open to sea spray, insist on leaving your bike somewhere else. Once you've been allocated your spot, you'll find there's normally a plate of raised steel set about eight inches out from the hull. I think it's there to save cars from clouting the steel plating, but it's also very convenient to stop your bike tumbling over. Quickly fasten your frame to something solid nearby, using a toe strap or elasticated hooks. I say quickly because if you hesitate a crew member will do the job for you with a bit of oily rope.

You then have the run of the ship until you berth. Note that you won't be able to return to the car deck once the ship has set sail, so take with you not only any valuables but anything you may need on board. Make a note of which deck you're on, and which side, otherwise you'll be fighting the crowd of motorists, lorry drivers and duty-free day trippers in a journey of exploration and frustration. To make this job easier, I notice, Sealink have started identifying decks not only by numbers but by pictures of elephants, whales, swans and who knows what else.

At the other end, just reclaim your bike, inch as far towards the exit as you can, and ride off with the cars. If anybody starts his car engine before it's needed, shout; otherwise you'll be drenched in exhaust fumes. Go straight to the front of the queue for passports (a minimal check in France and Belgium and usually only cursory in Holland, provided you've got an EEC passport) and customs. Nobody seems to object and some officials get cross if you don't. And pedal away. REMEMBER THAT YOU'RE NOW TRAVELLING ON THE RIGHT.

Ferry operators

P & O European Ferries (which now includes Townsend-Thoresen) are at 127 Regent Street, London W1R 8LB (01–734 4431) and the port reservation numbers are: Dover – 0304–203388; Portsmouth – 0705–827677; Felixstowe – 0394–604802.

Sealink, now owned by an American but still strongly connected with British

Rail, are at Eastern Docks, Dover, Kent CT16 1JA, and the number for reservations is 01–834 8122 or 0304–206090.

Brittany Ferries timetables are available by telephoning 0705–751708 or 0752–269926 (both 24-hour services); the numbers for reservations are Portsmouth 0705–827701; Plymouth 0752–221321; Cork 277801.

North Sea Ferries are at King George Dock, Hebdon Road, Hull, North Humberside HU9 5QA, and the telephone number is 0482–795141.

Olau Line are at Sheerness, Kent ME12 1SN, telephone 0795–666666.

Sally Line are at Ramsgate, Kent, where you can reach them on 0843–595522.

The most popular services are undoubtedly from Dover, and you can get a general guide for all services from Dover – up to 170 a day in the summer – from the Harbour Board, Harbour House, Dover, Kent CT17 9BU (telephone 0304–206560). If you have to stay overnight in Dover before crossing, the Dover Guest House Association operates a central bookings service on 0304–212512.

Hovercraft

The procedure for a hovercraft is exactly the same as for a ferry, except that bookings are essential. Flights are much less frequent than ferry crossings and they're also prone to disruption in bad weather, in which case they'll put you on the ship anyway. Remember that hovercraft don't depart from the ship docks, although at Dover the access is at the same place as Western Docks. In France, they're fairly remote from the town centre and the ship docks.

If you travel Seaspeed, inquire whether there is still a rebate for CTC members.

TRAIN AND FERRY

The novelty of a foreign holiday is the foreign bit, not the ride to the port at this end. Therefore there's an attraction in booking your bike in London and collecting it again at your holiday destination. Between the two, you're free to wander about in ordinary clothing, without everyone wondering why you're wearing a tracksuit and walking peculiarly in cycling shoes.

But life ain't that easy. What happens is that the bike makes the same journey as you but at different times, and very much more slowly if you have to cross a major town. You will go from Victoria to Dover, sail to Calais, join another train to Paris, cross Paris by metro or taxi, and take the overnight train to Nice, say. All very simple. The bike will probably go on the same train as far as Dover and will most likely cross the Channel with you. There is then some doubt as to whether it will make the same train to Paris. It will certainly not make the same train to Nice. Instead, it will reach the transit shed at the first Paris station and stay there until it's loaded on to a lorry or another train for the departure station. This takes a long time – certainly longer than your own journey across Paris – and it will be up to three days later that your bike finally joins you in Nice. Not a satisfactory situation unless you can send your bike several days in advance and you don't mind waiting for it again when you get home.

Travel agents know very little about registering bikes for foreign travel, so you might do best by dealing directly with British Rail's European Travel Centre at Victoria Station, London SW1V 1JY. The number for inquiries is 01–834 2345 (there's often a delay, but calls are dealt with in sequence, so hang on). Dial 01–828 0892 for credit card bookings.

Larger stations keep folders giving international train and ferry times, but if you want to possess every bit of information you could possibly need, the thing to get is the Thomas Cook European Timetable. It costs about £5 and, although I've never seen one on sale, it's said you can buy one at larger stations. Alternatively, you can buy one directly from the timetable publishing office at Thomas Cook, PO Box 36, Peterborough PE3 6SB. The head office is in the Thorpe Wood area of Peterborough.

Registering your bike

There are two viable options. If you decide to register the bike in London, do so only as far as the capital in which you're changing trains, even if the change is made in the same terminus. In Paris, Brussels or wherever, re-claim the bike (allowing an hour) and then ride it to the next terminus. The chances are that you won't have to register it for the next section of the journey, because it'll be within the same country. If it isn't, you just repeat the procedure.

My experience, though, recommends avoiding registration altogether. Take London to Antwerp, for example. The normal procedure is to catch the boat train to either Dover or Folkestone, which is convenient. But you can't take a bike on the boat train without registering it. So, instead, take an ordinary train to Dover Priory or Folkestone Central, which you can do quite properly with your international ticket. Both stations are on the centre or inland side of the town and it's about a 15-minute ride to the docks, where you then board the ship along with the cars and lorries.

As I explained before, there's a big difference between the routine at Dover Western and Eastern docks. Ships from Western docks aren't car ferries, so here you *will* have to register your bike. You will also have to pay for it. From Eastern docks, the bike won't be registered and you will keep it under your own control. It might also travel free. Check the situation at Folkestone before you travel (there are fewer ships, and the crossing's longer anyway, so you might just as well go from Dover).

We have three docks close to France on our side, but there's only one port at Calais and one at Boulogne. Both are next to a railway station. Unfortunately, train ferries aren't called that for nothing, and they're the ones that make the connection on the other side. There are relatively few trains from the harbour station so, just as you rode from Folkestone Central or Dover Priory on the British side, so you'll have to cycle to the town station at Boulogne and Calais. Both are just a few minutes' ride but it's wise, at all foreign railway stations, to give yourself at least 20 minutes to go through the registration procedure.

French trains

French trains are either much simpler than their British equivalent when it comes to travelling by bike, or they're much more difficult. At its easiest, you need do no more than tell the ticket clerk that you've got a bike. On the other hand you might have to register, in which case you'll need the door marked *bagages* or *bagages (consigne)*. The fee is standard, regardless of distance, and it's absolutely crucial that you don't lose your receipt. It's supposed to be the Germans who are keen on official forms, but the French can run them pretty close. Present the receipt at your destination, *bagages* or *bagages (arrivée)*. In the unlikely event that you turn up after your bike, you'll be expected to pay left-luggage charges. So, if you're sending your bike in advance, label it that way – *à l'avance* – and you won't get charged.

The situation and the routes vary just as they do in Britain, so the place to ask is the French Railways office in London (179 Piccadilly, London W1V 0BA; telephone 01–493 9731). Ask for the folder entitled *Guide du train et du vélo*. Just recently, French Railways started four trains for cyclists from Boulogne. You can, incidentally, hire bikes from SNCF, as well as other operators, especially in coastal areas. Sometimes they're pretty ordinary, at times they're lightweights. Ask SNCF for their leaflet *Train à Vélo*.

Belgian and Dutch trains

I've never had any trouble travelling with a bike in Belgium and Holland. You can't take a bike on a TEE, Trans-European Express, without crossing a national boundary (or *shouldn't*, anyway; Belgian rail officials once stopped a TEE at one wayside station and told it to stop at another, a few miles on, simply because the scheduled train service had been shortened and the replacement bus couldn't accommodate my bike). You can go on any other train you like in Belgium (except the silly electric bus-trains and the coastal trams) and, with restrictions on rush hours and other busy periods such as the peak summer, wherever you like on the Dutch railways. You'll notice, at many Dutch stations, that the stairs have wooden wheel guides to help you wheel your bike. There are also bike parks – *rijwielstalling* – at most Dutch stations.

The charge on Belgian trains is quite modest, but Dutch trains are charged by distance and can get quite pricey. In both cases, you load the bike yourself. In Holland you buy a ticket for yourself and the bike at the ticket office, as you would in Britain. In Belgium, the ticket office sells a ticket for you and the luggage office sells tickets for the bike. The latter come in several parts, one of which will be for the bike itself, one for the guard and one for you.

Belgian railways are at 10 Greycote Place, London SW1P 1SB (telephone 01–222 8866), and Dutch railways share with the Dutch tourist office at 25–28 Buckingham Gate, London SW1E 6LD. Both hire bikes (*locations de vélo* if you're in southern Belgium, *fietsverhuur* if you're in Holland or northern Belgium.)

BY AIR

Travelling by air is complicated in quite a different way. All airlines take bikes on their services, but airports are always some way out of town and invariably along a very boring and busy road. Getting into big airports like Heathrow might be exciting beyond your taste, although Heathrow does actually have a separate tunnel for bike riders. A cycle path runs from the terminals to the Newport Road roundabout on the A4 main road.

All airlines take bicycles, usually within the baggage allowance of 20kg (44lb). A bike with baggage will usually fit within the limit.

Always arrive at least half an hour before check-in time and report to the relevant desk. The check-in clerk will normally ask you to deflate the tyres, remove the wheels, reverse the pedals and turn the handlebars sideways. This is the way bikes used to travel in the days of flying boats and DC3s. The point of getting to the check-in desk early is that, confronted by this demand to wield the spanners for half an hour, you can ask the clerk to contact the loading supervisor. Having been one, I can tell you that check-in clerks never get to see the aeroplanes. They just have their rules. The loaders aren't daft, though, and they're well aware that it's much easier to wheel a bicycle than it is to carry one. That's the way *they* prefer it, especially in the cramped insides of the plane. Planes once had small hatches for baggage, but hatches now are made big enough to take pallets loaded by fork-lift trucks – plenty big enough for complete bicycles.

On the few occasions when my polite request has failed – and most airlines are happy to oblige if you give them time – the most I've ever had to do was remove the front wheel and strap it to the side of the frame. This makes the bike only inches shorter, because the rear mudguard is still in place, and it makes it a good deal harder to manoeuvre. But it's a compromise.

Sometimes airline officials who haven't heard that aircraft holds are pressurized ask for the tyres to be deflated. If you don't do it, someone else will, so all you can do is shrug. Don't let out all the air, though, because a bike bounced on flat tyres can get a dozen little nips in the inner tubes where they're squashed against the rim. Any check-in clerk who insists you reverse the pedals should be invited to try for him- or herself.

Some transatlantic airlines now ask for bikes to be packed in cardboard boxes, either yours or possibly one that they'll rent to you. It's a nuisance but it's better than taking things to bits. It's also probably safer for the bike; you might want to tape newspaper around the more prominent paintwork if it's travelling unwrapped. If you can't get a box at the airport – and ask before you book – try your local bike shop. Dealers get new machines from factories in boxes and will probably be glad to get rid of one.

The rules about baggage change frequently and different airlines often disagree. Some go by weight, some by size, some by size and weight. Collapsing the bike might save you some money if size is important; similarly, get the check-in clerk to weigh the bike if her guess is more than about 12 kilograms. Most officials accept 10 kilograms as a mutually acceptable estimate to save putting an awkward shape on scales made for suitcases. Otherwise, all you can do is check the airline's rules.

Do let the airline know in advance if you're travelling in a party of several bike riders. And remember that the rules which apply to bicycles don't apply to tandems or tricycles – in those cases you most certainly have to negotiate in advance and probably pay extra. If you have any doubts at all, ask the airline to confirm arrangements for your bike in writing. Airlines never have their head office at the airport, so the helpful employee who helped you on the phone will be quite unobtainable once you have a snag at the check-in desk. A letter on airline notepaper can work wonders.

Most airports have customs sheds, which mean your bike and luggage can be transferred right through to the final destination. This can be good news because it's then the rules of the first airline that apply, even though the second airline might want to charge for the bike. Luggage doesn't often go astray, but I have had two unfortunate experiences. Once I saw that BEA had labelled my bike 'Edinburgh to Malta' instead of 'Edinburgh to London' (I worked at Heathrow at the time, for BEA, and nabbed it before I lost it). On another occasion my luggage arrived at Birmingham from Cork, although the pump entrusted to Aer Lingus didn't complete the journey. The colleen at Cork airport (Irish translation, *aerophort*), had insisted on deflating the tyres. Without a pump, I couldn't ride the 60 miles home from Birmingham. The valves, unfortunately, were narrow, high-pressure ones and even a good-hearted search of the British Airways staff bike sheds couldn't produce a specialist pump to cope. British Airways weren't to be defeated and wheeled out two huge gas tanks used for inflating jumbo tyres. Sadly, that didn't work either and they took care of the bike while I travelled home by train.

Moral: don't rely on strapping your pump to your bags when you check them in separately, and consider insurance. The airline's compensation might well be less than it costs to carry out repairs to a damaged bike. I certainly got nothing for an enforced train ride.

A further note of caution. Do check, if your air journey involves a change of plane, whether you're expected to re-claim your bike at the transit point and re-register it. This can happen if you arrive at a main airport and fly on to a small provincial one.

IMPORT PROBLEMS

You can take a bike without problem into almost every country in the world, but most countries take a dim view of accepting more bikes than there are riders. In other words, if you drive to your foreign country, don't carry more bikes than there are people in the car or the customs people will assume you're trying to sell them.

I ran into this problem when driving from Czechoslovakia to the French coast after the world championships, carrying two competitors' bikes. All went well until I reached the French border from Belgium, where French customs officials conducted a lengthy explanation of Common Market rules about carrying only your own belongings across national frontiers.

Similarly, on going into some countries behind the Iron Curtain and elsewhere, you may be asked to register the bike, or to have its presence noted on your visa. On leaving the country you'll be asked to show as many bicycles as you brought in! The same could apply to mundane things like typewriters and cameras, although it's rarely a problem.

The most obvious nations to visit are those closest to the British coast. In fact, there are slight differences in the rules concerning entry into western European countries which are and aren't members of the Common Market, but the variations are too small to worry about. None of the western European countries requires any special conditions for cycles or their riders.

PASSPORTS AND VISAS

There is, fortunately, a worldwide trend against visas and entry permits. Common Market nationals have the right of free passage throughout Common Market nations. But although strictly speaking the Treaty of Rome doesn't insist you carry a passport (just everyday identification), the truth is that you won't get very far without one.

There is no set pattern to those nations which require a visa from other country's nationals. If you've got any doubts, ring either the embassy or the national travel agency of the country concerned.

When you get really adventurous and decide to wander across several borders in one holiday, the trick is to apply for your visas in reverse order, because many nations won't give you an entry visa until you've secured a way out and into the neighbouring nation. It's not often that you'll run into a problem in obtaining what you want (unless you have, say, a South African, Israeli or Egyptian passport and you pick a country which doesn't like your leaders), but it can be a time-consuming and occasionally a moderately expensive one.

Some nations, like Czechoslovakia, insist that you change a set amount of hard currency each day for local money, and money-changers board the train at the border for just this purpose. On the other hand, as I found, you can change whatever's left when you leave the country again.

There are just a few countries which won't allow you in at all – Albania was one for many years. And the Soviet Union will let you in with a welcome, but not if you want to go off cycling – although, there again, things seem to be changing.

MONEY PROBLEMS

Although there's a move towards a common currency for all the Common Market countries – businessmen already have the ecu – it seems many decades off yet. Therefore you've got to be prepared.

Luckily, things are much easier than they were. Once there was no alternative but to take wads of foreign currency and then telegraph (there were no international phone lines) for your domestic bank to send more. Then came travellers' cheques, which are still around. And then came the European banking system and credit cards.

Travellers' cheques are by no means as convenient or as cheap as the advertising makes them seem. You have to buy them in the first place, you have to pay commission on them, and you have to exchange them at the other end. You can hold them in most currencies, but it doesn't mean that the currency you hold is the one that the other nation wants. So you pay extra commission. If you go to the United States – basically if you go outside Europe – then travellers' cheques become more attractive. But these days it's a lot easier to rely on Eurocheques and credit cards inside Europe.

Eurocheques are just ordinary bank cheques made to a design recognized by banks all over Europe. You fill them in a slightly different way (the value comes before the name, and the date's in a different place) but apart from that they're exactly the same. Order them from your bank, along with a Eurocheque card, before you leave.

You can use the cheques anywhere you might ordinarily write a cheque. There's a space on the back for you to write the number of the guarantee card, and space on the front for you to enter the currency, since the joy of a Eurocheque is that you can write it in any European currency. The cheques go back through the bank system and they're deducted from your balance, although you still pay commission on the currency transfer.

Credit cards aren't as common in continental Europe as they are in Britain and, especially, in the United States. The easiest to use is Barclaycard, which is known throughout Europe as Visa and, in France, as Carte Bleue (Carte Bleue is actually a French firm, but it too has a link with Visa and therefore it's the colloquial name). The next easiest is Access, but many people don't recognize that it's part of the Eurocard and Mastercharge set-up. Once you've pointed that out, you should have no trouble.

It's not easy to pay everyday bills on credit in Holland. In France it's better, and even easier to pay by cheque, because French law makes it illegal to refuse a cheque (when proferred by a Frenchman, anyway) and makes it a grave offence to offer a bouncing cheque. In some countries, like Spain, your Eurocheque card will withdraw money from the hole-in-the-wall machine.

If you *do* run out of money, ring your bank at home, explain the situation and name a bank to which you'd like to have money transferred. This can happen in a few hours, especially if you use what your own bank calls its 'correspondent' bank in the country you're in. That's a system of co-operation that all banks have with their counterparts abroad.

Finally, if you're absolutely on your uppers, the British embassy will help. But not willingly. Going to the embassy for help is really the last measure and they certainly won't smile on you. The money, if it's forthcoming at all, will be only a loan. They might want proof you can repay it; they might want security.

Tell them you want advice rather than money, though, and they will be very relieved, smile sweetly and help you find your own way out of a fix.

II. Country by Country

The trouble with abroad, says an old Fenland friend, is that the mountains get in the way of the view. These particular obstructions are the French Alps.

Austria

Austria is a dramatic country with equally dramatic gradients. In the east it starts to flatten out, but only then in relation to the mountains. You can, if you want a good hard ride, tackle the country's highest pass, the Gross Glockner, at 3,797 metres. The main mountain passes are smooth and evenly-paced, though, which is a small consolation, although minor roads in backwoods areas can still be rough or loosely surfaced.

Austria is twice the size of Switzerland but has only the same population. At the same time, one in four Austrians lives in Vienna, which leaves a lot of room everywhere else for you and your bike. Because of that, it's a great country for off-road riding, with easy tracks and tough tracks to choose from.

Language

Austrians speak German but view Germans with wry amusement, seeing them in the same stereotypes as outsiders – over-formal, over-industrious, slightly unimaginative – but with the added sharpness of having them as not entirely dissimilar neighbours. No one seems odder than someone *almost* like yourself. Austrians, by and large, don't speak English outside the big cities and tourist haunts.

Accommodation

You should have no trouble finding somewhere to stay. There are country inns and small hotels (*Gasthof* or *Gasthaus*), the distinction being that a *Gasthof* will *always* have rooms to let and the *Gasthaus* often will. There are also private rooms roughly of the British type. Look out for signs advertising *Zimmer Frei* or *Fremdenzimmer* or *Privat Zimmer* or *Fremdenheime*. The big difference is that food isn't always provided. Generally you'll get a simple breakfast, but rarely an evening meal.

Local tourist offices are called *Verkehrsverein* and they're often at the railway station. Write to them in advance and they might well send you a list of all accommodation in the area.

Austria has plenty of youth hostels which are not evenly spread throughout the country and are usually small and quite full, particularly in high season. Most are south of the Danube and in the Salzkammergut, and the big towns have several. But elsewhere they're a long way apart.

Camping is easy if you don't insist on a formal site. There are, in fact, a good number of sites but they follow the youth hostel principle of crowding themselves into small areas, like the Tyrol and Salzkammergut, and are often crowded. Elsewhere they're a good spread apart, although with so much of Austria being 'wild', you should have no trouble pitching a small tent somewhere. Try to find the landowner to ask permission, but don't be surprised if there's no house within miles.

Cycling

Cycle paths are compulsory. Beware of Viennese trams. There are relatively few roads in Austria and they're busy in late July and August and whenever there's a public holiday in Germany.

Bike shops are rare outside Vienna and a few other towns, although garages will sometimes help with disasters and there's often a cycle department in sports shops. Apart from that, it's up to you.

Weather

As you'd expect from the pictures in tourist books, Austria has cold and snowy winters and mild, frequently sunny summers. It's hard to pick a prevailing wind because it's so often broken by the mountains, but if anything it blows from the west.

Summers aren't dry. Austria has showers rather than persistent summer rain or drizzle, but remember that June, July and August are the wettest months.

Snow lasts from late December until late March in the mountains, and for a further month once you get above 6,000 feet (1,830 metres). Snow is more or less permanent from 2,500 metres upwards. Mountain passes are gated at the bottom when they're impassable.

Public transport

You can take your bike on trains for a set fee which doesn't change with distance. Avoid registering your bike because it costs twice as much and can take three days to travel even a short way. There's a good train network and you can reach almost anywhere in the country that's not high up a mountain. The trains aren't always fast, though, because of the mountains.

The Austrian tourist office publishes a leaflet, *Fahrrad am Bahnhof*, listing which stations will rent you a bike.

You can also take a bike on some buses.

Maps

Michelin publish a map of Austria in one sheet (no. 426) at 1:400,000 (1 centimetre equals 4 kilometres). It's too small for everyday cycling but good for planning because the mountains are well marked and the scenic roads are picked out in green. There's also a Holzel map at 1:600,000.

The best maps for riding while you're there though are the Mair general series (*Die General Karte*) at 1:200,000. It covers the country in eight sheets. There are town plans on the back.

For more detailed exploration, and particularly for off-road riding, look for the *Wanderkarten* maps published by Freytag and Berndt. They're 1:100,000 (1 centimetre to 1 kilometre), which is good enough to show even footpaths. Heights are indicated by colour shading. There are 52 sheets to the whole country, so you do need to know just which bit you're visiting if you don't want to carry the whole library.

Useful addresses

Austrian National Tourist Office, 30 St George's Street, London W1R 9FA (01–629 0461).
Österreichischer Fahrradverband (the organization for non-competitive cycling), Hasnerstrasse 10, 1160 Vienna.

The various youth hostel organizations are:
Österreichischer Jugendherbergsverband, Schottenring 28, 1010 Vienna (635353)
Österreichischer Jugendherbergswerk, Freyung 6/11, 1010 Vienna (631833)
Österreichischer Jugendferienwerk, Alpenstrasse 08a, 5020 Salzburg (257850).

Currency

The *schilling*.

Other information

Republic, capital: Vienna. 83,853 square kilometres (32,376 square miles). Population: 7,750,000.

Belgium

Belgium is the oddest country in Europe and, if it didn't already exist, nobody would find a need to invent it. It's endlessly flat in the north, hilly in the south and mountainous in the south-east. It is, though, a country to whom cyclists are no strangers, even if the side roads aren't always kind. It's a crowded country and main roads are invariably busy, even though they'll have a cycle lane or path beside them. The lanes are pleasant, with surfaces that vary from excellent to viciously cobbled.

Language

Belgium has three official languages – Dutch (called Flemish for nationalistic reasons) in the north, French in the south, and a tiny area in the extreme east where German is a protected minority language. Draw a line just south of Brussels and the Dutch-speaking area of Flanders lies to the north and the French region of Wallonia to the south. Brussels has French and Dutch suburbs but its working language is French, even though it's in Flanders.

The thing to remember is that Belgium *isn't* bi-lingual. Flemings invariably speak French and, almost as invariably, English. But both are foreign languages to them and, for a couple of reasons, many would rather speak English than French. Use your French if it's obviously good, but do explain first that you're British or American or whatever. For many years the French language dominated Belgium and many Flemings still feel resentful about using it. There's a strong nationalistic feeling and some are reluctant to speak French to Walloons.

This is made doubly difficult because the Walloons, in turn, consider that it is they who have the world language and that the Flemings speak not only a minor language but speak it, generally, rather badly – which is true. They therefore refuse to learn it. Since they're also not terribly good at speaking anything else, you must expect to speak French (with a few local variations, such as the numbers; 80 is not *quatre-vingts* but *huitante*; 90 is *nonante*).

Road signs are written in the prevailing local language, so beware of changes along the linguistic border. The most prevalent are:

In English	In Dutch	In French
Antwerp	Antwerpen	Anvers
Bruges	Brugge	Bruges
Brussels	Brussel	Bruxelles
Ghent	Gent	Gand
Grammont	Geraardsbergen	Grammont
Kortrijk	Kortrijk	Courtrai
Liege	Luik	Liège
Louvain	Leuven	Louvain
Mechelen	Mechelen	Malines
Mons	Bergen	Mons
Namur	Namen	Namur
Roubaix	Rijsel	Roubaix
Tirlemont	Tienen	Tirlemont
Ypres	Ieper	Ypres

Accommodation

There's no shortage anywhere of inexpensive, if shabby, hotels. Towns are close together, so you rarely have far to ride. Avoid staying in Brussels unless you have a lot of money or use one of the youth hostels there.

Most towns have a tourist office: *Dienst voor Toerisme* in the north, *Syndicats d'Initiative* in the south.

There's no accommodation in private homes. There is, however, a good network of youth hostels, run by several organizations: the Vlaamse Jeugdher-bergcentral and the Centrale Wallonne des Auberges de la Jeunesse. Both belong to the IYHA and your domestic card is valid at all their hostels. These follow the national traits, so that Flemish hostels tend to the German norm: large buildings and greater organisation while the Walloons go for smaller buildings and less noticeable order.

This, again, being Belgium, there are several other groups offering hostel-type accommodation, without youth hostel rules, and also a few independent free spirits. The main ones are: Centre Belge de Tourisme des Jeunes, Rue Guimard 1, 1040 Bruxelles (512.54.47); Les Amis de la Nature, Rue de l'Enseignement 24, 4800 Verviers (33.05.45); Centrum voor Jeugdtoerisme, Diestestraat 235, 3000 Leuven (22.65.30); Het Natuurvriendenhuis, Provincie-straat 53, 2000 Antwerpen (36.18.62).

To save you writing to each individually, the Belgian national tourist office in London (see 'Useful addresses') keeps lists of all hostels, affiliated and otherwise.

Wild camping is just about possible in some parts of Flanders, and legally frowned upon. Private land is considered very much private, as you'll see from the prevalence of signs, and open fields are intensively farmed. Unfortunately, official sites – of which there are about 500 – aren't evenly spread. You'll find them along the coast and in the Ardennes but not easily elsewhere.

Cycling

Roads vary in quality, although principal routes are generally good. Cycle paths are compulsory; note that they can sometimes be shared stretches of pavement. Look out for the path being switched across the road for no real reason in the country. Look out, too, for trams and tramlines in cities like Antwerp.

You'll never see a country with as many quality bike shops as Belgium. Every village of any size will have at least one, some even opening on Sunday mornings to handle the leisure trade. Just ask anywhere you happen to be for the nearest *fietsenwinkel* or for *bicyclettes.*

Belgian cyclists pay tax on their bikes and have to have front, rear and pedal reflectors. As a tourist, you're spared from this rule, but you are expected to take your passport with you wherever you go.

Belgium closes early at night, so eat before 6 pm if you're journeying on.

Otherwise the best you'll find are expensive restaurants and cheap chip vans (*frituur* in Dutch).

Weather

Belgian weather is similar to neighbouring Britain's, with slightly warmer summers and chillier winters. A great deal of the country is scarcely above sea level, though, which means there's nothing to stop the wind, which can be both cold and hard work. Mists are common in the early morning but soon clear.

Public transport

Belgium has an excellent rail network and most trains take bikes. See the previous chapter. There are also buses between towns and long-distance trams, or light railways, along the coast. Neither takes bicycles. The country is too small for internal air services, although there are numerous airports.

Maps

The only practical choice is the Michelin yellow-fronted series at 1:200,000. It shows all the roads you'll want to ride on and several that you wish (when you find the cobbles) you hadn't found.

Useful addresses

Belgian National Tourist Office, Premier House, 2 Gayton Road, Harrow, Middlesex HA1 2XU (01–861 3300).

Belgische Wielrijdersbond/Ligue Vélocipédique Belge (the national cycling body, although concerned mainly with racing). In Dutch the address is Globelaan 49, 1190 Brussel; in French it's Avenue de Globe 49, 1190 Bruxelles. Both are exactly the same place and the telephone number is 343.00.08.

SNCB (the railway company), rue de France 85, 1070 Brussels; and 10 Greycote Place, London SW1P 1SB (01–222 8866).

Currency

The franc or frank, written Fr and divided into 100 largely useless and unobtainable coins called centimes. Belgian money is accepted in Luxemburg, and is of equal value, but it doesn't work the other way round.

Other information

Kingdom, capital: Brussels. Total area: 30,519 square kilometres (11,784 square miles). Population: 10,000,000.

Denmark

Denmark is a gentle country, not unlike East Anglia. It's low and it's undemanding – the highest road is just 171 metres – but it's not flat, certainly not as flat as Holland. That, and the fact that it's so small – not only because there's not much of it but because what there is is divided among numerous islands – make it quite unlike the other Scandinavian countries.

You'll find plenty of small lanes – and several busy, flat, windy and monotonous main roads. The lanes are well surfaced, but watch out for stretches of cobbles in towns.

The Danes, like other Scandinavians, have a refreshing attitude to private land. Put simply, the law allows you to ride on private land in daylight, provided you stay to existing paths and tracks and provided the wood or park is larger than five hectares (about nine acres, or the size of ten British football pitches).

Language

The national language is Danish which, when written at least, you can make a few guesses at, if you know anything of German or Dutch. Like the Dutch, though, they've accepted that they've got a little-spoken language and most Danes speak good English.

Accommodation

There's a good chain of youth hostels, about ninety of them scattered evenly throughout the country. They're well equipped and of a high standard. There are few bed-and-breakfast establishments and the hotels, except those run by the YMCA, are expensive. But somewhere in the middle of the two is the *kro*, which you'd never guess meant 'inn'. It's also possible to stay in farmhouses, especially by booking in advance through an organized holiday scheme.

Most towns have a tourist centre – *Touristbureauet* – to help with accommodation and information.

Camping's fairly simple provided you don't want to camp wild. Denmark is too heavily cultivated and too populous to make that easy. The signs *Teltslagning Forbudt* and *Ingen Camping* mean no camping. There are 500 approved sites, well scattered, of which a shade more than a tenth stay open in the winter. Standards are high and sites are graded. If you haven't got a camping *Carnet*, you'll be asked to buy a Danish camping permit at the first site you visit. The big map shops in Britain stock the guide to Danish sites published by the Danish Camping Committee.

There's no trouble finding somewhere to eat, but it's usually expensive. Better to carry your own midday meal and eat out in the evening.

Cycling

The most important difference involves turning left. Instead of moving out to the centre of the road, the rule is to stay on the right as far as the junction, wait for a gap in the road, and then cross directly into the side turning.

Unlike almost everywhere else in Europe, the Danes ride 26- and 27-inch wheels. They ride metric wheels as well, but at least you should be able to buy a spare tyre without trouble. There are also plenty of bike shops; Danes see cycling as a normal way of getting about.

Weather

Both winters and summers are short, so that Denmark has the illusion of being permanently in early spring. Otherwise it's much like southern Britain, mild, a bit damp (but not wet, since the hills are too low to provoke the clouds) and unremarkable, but with spring actually arriving a bit later.

Public transport

You can hire bikes at a few railway stations but the service isn't widespread. Nor does it run all year. It's not a thing to rely on.

Nor does the Danish national railway company, the DSB, smile on cyclists beyond that. You can't, for example, take your bike on a train without registering it first and wondering when it'll turn up at your destination. It's a bit easier on the handful of trains run by private companies, but the situation varies, so check in advance by ringing the station.

Ferries, on the other hand, are much simpler – and often free. That's just as well in a country which depends on its shipping links.

Maps

Best by far is the *Cykelseriekort*, published by the Danish cycle campaigners, Dansk Cyklist Forbund. I've never found one for sale in Britain, so write to the DCF at Kjeld Langes Gade 14, 1367 Copenhagen K. The telephone number is Copenhagen 144212. It shows cycle paths, recommended routes and much else besides. There's also a wealth of information on the back, all in English.

For a larger scale, go for the GI (Geodœtisk Institut) maps at 1:200,000 or 1:100,000. The smaller scale is probably better because just three or four maps cover the whole country, whereas you need a saddlebag-full of the others.

Useful addresses

Danish tourist board, Sceptre House, 169–173 Regent Street, London W1R 8PY (01–734 2637) or Olof Palmes Gade 10, 2100 Copenhagen 0 (423222).

Dansk Cyklist Forbund (the national campaigning and, by implication, cycle touring, organization), Kjeld Langes Gade 14, 1367 Copenhagen K (144212).
DSB (Danish state railways), Banegårdspladsen, 1570 Copenhagen V.

Currency

The krone.

Other information

Kingdom, capital: Copenhagen. 43,075 square kilometres (16,631 square miles). Population: 5,250,000.

Finland

If Belgium is the oddest country in Europe, it's Finland that has the most obscure language. It makes sense to Finns but to everyone else it looks as though the words are written with all the letters that other languages left out.

It's not a wonderful cycling country. It's remote and peaceful, but it's also much the same for hundreds of miles on end. In the main that means flat countryside with plenty of water and trees.

To make things worse, Finland is in almost permanent winter compared to most of the Continent. Summer – surprisingly warm – is just a slip of mind in the middle of the year.

Language

Don't even attempt to understand Finnish unless you're committed to mastering difficult and useless languages. Nor does everyone share the Scandinavian love of speaking English – they do in the cities but not much elsewhere. But then, there aren't many Finns elsewhere anyway. Many Finns also speak Swedish, if that's a consolation.

Accommodation

There's quite a range of youth hostels, mostly in the south but also enough beyond the Arctic circle to make adventure a possibility. There are also a lot of campsites, again in the warmer south, and often by lakes. Finns themselves like staying in farmhouses and purpose-built cabins in woods.

Tourism is reasonably well developed and larger towns have information offices (*Matkailutoimisto*). Don't, by the way, confuse tourist offices with travel agents, which have the similar name of *Matkatoimisto.*

Cycling

The roads – and there's a good range of minor ones – are where the people are – in the south. Further north there are just the main roads that strike into unknown territory. Road surfaces vary, from good to dust, but even the worst are ridable, if bumpy.

You'll find bike shops in the biggest cities, and sometimes stocking a few lightweight bits and pieces, but apart from that you're on your own. Note that although the Finns aren't strangers to imperial-sized wheels, you might have trouble finding 27-inch tyres.

Weather

A long cold winter and a brief, warm summer with unbelievably long days. It stays light all night in the north, in a hazy sort of way. Generally, it'll get no warmer in summer than it does in southern England.

Public transport

It's worth using a train to knock off long distances that might otherwise make undistinguished cycling. All but the fastest and most local trains take bikes, although not as accompanied luggage. The usual problems exist of sending a bike on a different train from yourself, but given the country, the aggravation becomes more worthwhile. Send the bike ahead of you if you can – book it in one day and you should get it the next.

There are air services between Helsinki and the major provincial cities.

Maps

Look for the Hallweg 1:1,000,000 which, given the sparseness of the country, will probably suffice. Otherwise the Suomen Tiekartta maps at 1:200,000 cover the nation in nineteen sheets, with as much and probably more information than you need.

Useful addresses

Finnish Tourist Board, 66 Haymarket, London SW1Y 4RE (01–839 4048).
Finnish Cycling Association (the organization for touring cyclists), Radrokatu 12,
   PL27, 00241 Helsinki.

Currency

The mark (FM).

Other information

Republic (called Suomi), capital: Helsinki. 337,032 square kilometres (130,129 square miles).
Population: 4,800,000.

France is the most varied and, in my opinion, the most beautiful country in Europe. It's around three times the size of Britain with only a similar population.

Road surfaces are generally good, roads are empty and French drivers, contrary to legend, are good to cyclists.

It's impossible to summarize a country which has as many regions as Britain plus as many variations again. But if you have to try, it's a fair generalization to say that the north and north-east are rolling, extremely open, calm, misty and rather dull; the centre stretch from Paris to Poitiers is monoculture; Brittany is dramatic with hidden villages and tough climbs; the south-west is flat and sandy near the coast, with large stretches of pine forest and splendid beaches, the area from Poitiers southwards ranges from rolling to hilly, with beautiful scenery but busier roads (particularly in the Dordogne valley, where you'll notice most 'GB' plates); the south-east centre is hilly and sparse; the east is mountainous because of the Alps, and the Mediterranean stretch is warm (and windy when the mistral blows), sometimes dull, often beautiful, nearly always crowded.

The French, despite their government trying to make them do otherwise, nearly all go on vacation in July and August, especially where the two months meet. Apart from then, France is great to visit at any time. In the south, you could even be wearing shorts in early March . . . if you're lucky.

Language

French is, so the French insist, every bit as much a world language as English. Therefore they are about as bad as English-speakers at learning (or at least remembering) foreign languages.

The language they speak varies from north to south, being lazier in the south, with words like *douze* (twelve) being pronounced *dooz-uh* rather than the Parisian *dooze*. Those aberrations aside, French is the common language and you either have to speak it or go largely not understood.

In those areas such as Brittany and the south-west, where a few people still speak older, native languages (Bretagne and Oc, respectively), they'll switch happily to French for your benefit.

Accommodation

The thrill about accommodation in France is that it's both plentiful and inexpensive. Bed-and-breakfast, although now just starting in France, is to all purposes non-existent. The nearest equivalent is *chambre-d'hôte*, which in theory should be a room in a large house but sometimes proves to be no more than a hotel room. But there are endless campsites and cheap hotels.

The thing to remember with hotels is that the charge is by the room, not by the person. Therefore the price tumbles if there are two or three of you. Customarily, you'll be shown the room before being asked to agree and, in some cases, this isn't a bad idea. There are bad hotels in France just as there are everywhere else. However, the French seem to take less offence at having their offered rooms rejected.

Prices are displayed in the room by law and don't include breakfast. The *patron* might well expect you to eat at the hotel, not necessarily at great expense, it being on the meal rather than the room that he's making his money.

French bars have to have their prices hanging on display. To get that price, though, you need to stand at the bar and ask for anything listed in exactly the way that it is listed. Any variation, such as asking for a Pernod rather than a *pastis*, or taking a seat, attracts a higher price. It's certainly not the thing to buy at bar prices and then sit down, as the *patron* will assuredly and volubly explain.

The best place for information on any topic in a French town is the *Syndicat d'Initiative* – if it's open, which isn't always the case. Remember that the French tend to stop for the night earlier than other Europeans and that rooms will start filling quickly in tourist areas. The *Syndicat* will also point you towards campsites, of which the French have a great number. Registered sites are shown on Michelin maps with a black triangle in brackets but there are many more besides. The cheapest and simplest are municipal campsites, but even the best equipped are inexpensive. Wild camping is allowed, but not encouraged in areas such as the valleys running down to the Mediterranean which have been burned bare of trees by careless campers.

If you're looking for a permanent site for centre touring, try booking a gîte, either through one of the big agencies such as Bowhill's (Swanmore, Southampton, Hants SO3 2QW; 0489–877627) or through the French organizations listed in the address section. Gîtes are as varied as British youth hostels, but otherwise quite unlike them. They're country houses, sometimes converted barns, sometimes well-furnished but basic, sometimes equipped with swimming pools. The level of luxury you choose is up to you, but never will you be slumming it and rarely will you be disappointed. Added to that, charges are often independent of the number of people staying (although the exact terms vary from company to company).

There are 170 affiliated youth hostels (*auberges de la jeunesse*) in France and numerous independent ones. They all go by the same name and there seems no rule by which to guess which will be sumptuous and which will be frankly, dreadful.

Cycling

If France has a fault, it's the Napoleonic one of tackling hills straight on. Only in the toughest regions will roads so much as snake up hills, let alone go round them. The effect is that you'll find yourself dropping down through the gears as drags go on seemingly endlessly.

Road surfaces are good except perhaps for the tiniest by-ways and for some towns in the north, which still have stretches of cobbles. France has come a long way in the last decade and a half and all the horror stories, if they were ever true, are a thing of the past.

The main roads are often busy, especially with loaded trucks, which would have to pay hefty tolls on the *autoroutes*. A scheme called the Wily Bison diverts as much traffic as it can on to secondary roads in high summer, but even that shouldn't trouble you too much if you stick to the lanes. The consistent bad spots are the mountain climbs in the Alps and Pyrenees, where all the traffic is crammed on to narrow and sometimes unfenced roads. It takes nerve to hold your place when you're sandwiched between a Spanish truck and a sheer drop. My advice is keep clear of the mountains in July and August.

Cycle paths (*Piste cyclable obligatoire*) are compulsory – where they exist. French cyclists rarely use battery lights and you'll never see a Sturmey Archer gear, so you won't find spares, but there are plenty of bike shops, and even garages will lend a hand. French bikes are idiosyncratic and have odd threads. Imperial-sized wheels are unknown and if you haven't got a pair of 26-inch wheels, which will just about double for a metric, treat yourself to a pair of 622- or 700-millimetre wheels and join a trend which is happening in Britain and the US anyway.

Weather

France ranges from the cold and misty Channel coast to the hot and sultry Mediterranean. As you'd expect, everything else fits somewhere along the scale between cold and hot. The two main exceptions are Provence, which can be windy, especially so when the mistral blows, and the Massif Central, which can be bleak, exposed and highly windy. It's a depressed area in more than an industrial sense.

Public transport

The main information for taking a bike by train in France is listed earlier. It's a bit more simple than in Britain, but not much. There is also a network of internal airlines, which will carry bikes happily but which aren't cheap to use.

Maps

There are two options: either the yellow-covered Michelin at 1:200,000 or the Institut Géographique National green maps at 1:100,000. The IGN maps are prettier but you get through a lot more if you're on the move.

Useful addresses

French Government Tourist Office, 178 Piccadilly, London W1V 0AL (01–491 7622).
SNCF (French railways), 179 Piccadilly, London W1V 0BA (01–493 9731).
Fédération Française de Cyclo-tourisme, 8 rue Jean-Marie Jego, 75013 Paris (580.30.21).
Fédération Nationale des Gîtes Ruraux de France, 34 rue Godot-de-Mauroy, 75009 Paris.
Fédération Nationale des Logis et Auberges de France, 25 rue Jean Mermoz, 75008 Paris.

Currency

The French franc, written F, is made up of 100 centimes. But whereas Britain decimalized its currency and got used to it within months, the French never got the hang of devaluation and the introduction of francs worth many times the old currency. Therefore, although the prices you'll see quoted in shops are in the 'new' currency (actually more than a decade old), even middle-aged people think in old francs. This is alarming if you're on the receiving end.

Watch out in shops for prices which don't include a comma (the Continental equivalent of a decimal point) between the francs and the centimes.

Other information

Republic, capital: Paris. 543,965 square kilometres (210,026 square miles). Population: 54,000,000.

Germany (West)

Germany, like France, is a big country with great differences north to south. It doesn't have the Mediterranean coast and it doesn't have the alps, but it does have something for most tastes. Sadly, it also has a great number of cars, this being the most automobile-besotted nation on the Continent. It also has great sprawling industrial and residential areas that link up the major cities, particularly in the north.

It is, though, a promising country for cycling and one which, *Autobahns* apart, is kind to cyclists.

Language

German, of course, with a distinct softening of the accent as you move south. A great many people speak English.

Accommodation

Accommodation is at the same time more available and better classified than anywhere else in Europe. Not so much as a patch of land for a sleeping bag seems to escape the Germanic enthusiasm for being graded according to luxury and facilities.

There are, for instance, more youth hostels than anywhere else, and they too are graded. They are also very large and organized. It was, after all, in Germany that the *Jugendherbergen* movement began. With sensible planning, all 550 are evenly spaced and evenly distributed. But, if you hated school parties at British hostels, you'll detest the German ones. Look instead for the rather less common independent hostels, the *Naturfreundehaus*, which can be as simple or as luxurious as a British hostel.

There are close on 2,500 campsites, which suits the Germans, who are great campers, ramblers and thigh-slappers. Facilities and organization are intense, and prices, as campsites go, are high. Much of Germany is too populous and too heavily farmed for wild camping, but it is possible in Bavaria. It's essential to ask the landowner for permission; Germany doesn't turn the blind eye that you might enjoy elsewhere.

Hotels can be wildly expensive, but there's a good alternative in inns and bed-and-breakfast accommodation. Inns are signed as *Gasthof* or *Gasthaus*. Next down the scale are *Fremdenzimmer* and *Pensionen*. Cheaper and friendlier yet are the bed-and-breakfast houses, for which you'll see *Zimmer* or *Zimmer frei* signs.

For help with accommodation, and almost anything else, look for the *Verkehrsämt*, the tourist office.

Cycling

Cycle paths are compulsory and frequently pretty sorry affairs. At times they'll force you to ride against the traffic, throwing you back across the road when the path dies out. Don't ride two-abreast.

Germans drive like maniacs, the only good point of that being that they accordingly prefer the bigger, straighter roads.

There are a fair number of bike shops and, until recently, you would have found it pretty easy to buy imperial-sized tyres. Now though it's harder, because German cyclists are going metric.

You can hire bikes at 250 railway stations during the summer.

Weather

There's not much difference in temperature north to south. As much as you'd expect things to warm up in the south, so the figures stay the same because the land gets higher. Summers are a few degrees warmer than in Britain, winters a little colder in the lowlands, several degrees colder in the mountains.

Public transport

You can take a bike by train on almost the same conditions as in Britain, although with fewer exceptions. The main exemptions are the fastest and the smallest trains. The train does have to have a luggage van, though. Buy a bike ticket and load the bike on the train yourself. The price is the same regardless of how far you go.

Maps

Germany keeps its history of separate provinces when it comes to maps – each region has its official cartographer.

The best standard map is the Mair *Deutsche Generalkarte* at 1:200,000, but it's expensive and you'll need twenty-five to cover the country. Michelin covers part of the country (the areas nearest to France) at a fraction of the cost, and at the same scale.

Useful addresses

German National Tourist Office, 65 Curzon Street, London W1Y 7PE (01–495 3990).
Algemeiner Deutscher Fahrrad-Club (the national campaigning organization and, by extension, the one with most interest in casual cyclists), Postfach 107744, 2800 Bremen 1.
Bund Deutscher Radfahrer (the national cycling body, mainly racing but also

touring), Otto-Fleck-Schneise 4, 6000 Frankfurt am Main 71.
German Camping Club, Mandlstrasse 28, 8000 Munich 23.

Currency

The mark or Deutschmark, written DM or M. The mark is divided into 100
Pfenningen. Note that the currency in East Germany, the GDR-M, is quite
different.

Other information

Federal republic, capital: Bonn. 248,667 square kilometres (96,011 square
miles). Population: 61,500,000. Note that West Germany also includes enclaves
of Berlin. Travel between the two usually presents little difficulty with a British
or an American passport, but it would be wise to check visa and currency
requirements before you go because they can change.

Italy

A cynic told me once that Italy is just like Norway. And so it is, I suppose, when
you think that it's about the same size, a similar shape, and they've both got a
great big mountain down the middle. Apart from that . . . well, apart from that,
they're totally different. The sun is one thing that comes to mind.

It's the mountain that makes Italy tough going. The coastal routes are busy,
and Italians live up to their reputation when it comes to driving. A right-angle
turn off the main road takes you slap bang into the mountains and over a pass.
It'll be an easier pass than in the Alps or the Pyrenees, but it's a pass
nevertheless.

Language

Italian, of course. And English isn't widely spoken. You might be able to get by
with some French and German.

Accommodation

There are countless campsites along the coast, frequently crowded in mid-
summer (which isn't a good time for cycling, anyway). Youth hostels are mainly

in the Po Valley and in the Lakes, but hotels and pensions are cheap and cheerful and should suffice for a whole tour. Be careful, though, because the price you are quoted doesn't necessarily include all the possible extra charges. Ask, unless you're prepared to spend more than you intended.

Cycling

Watch out for cobbles in the towns and for exceptionally busy and breakneck roads along the coast – unless the road is paralleled by an *autostrada*, in which case it'll be a lot quieter. You'll appreciate that, because every driver sees it as a duty to hoot at least once before overtaking.

Apart from cobbles and some gritty roads in the mountains, surfaces are generally adequate. The further south you go, the poorer the country and the worse the roads become.

Frankly, the roads hover between being exhilarating and downright dangerous. Never expect a motorist to give you the right of way; he might, he might not, so gamble that he won't. Cities like Milan, Rome and Turin aren't worth the misery of cycling in them.

Signposting is dreadful.

For all that Italians love cycling, they have no love for cycle touring. For them cycling is a competitive sport. That shows in the bike shops, which are very flashy and restricted mainly to large towns.

The good side is that there is plenty of off-road cycling up in the hills.

Weather

Italy ranges from warm to stinking hot, in proportion to how far south you go. The rain falls mainly in February and March.

Public transport

Most trains (but not the fastest) will take bikes. Buy a ticket about three-quarters of an hour before the train leaves and let the station staff put the bike on the train. Don't make short journeys by train because the cost of taking the bike is outrageous – several times more than your own ticket. The further you go, the cheaper, in comparison, the bike price becomes.

Maps

Use the Touring Club Italiano 1:200,000 maps, which are cumbersome but unsurpassed in Italy.

Useful addresses

Italian Government Travel Office, 1 Princes Street, London W1R 8AY (01–408 1254).
Touring Club Italiano, Corso Italia 10, 20122 Milan.

Currency

The lire, which by itself is so valueless that the coins are worth more in scrap metal than they are in currency. From time to time, therefore, someone takes it into his head to melt a load down and until the mint catches up, the country is reduced to accepting cigarettes and sticks of chewing gum as change. The government keeps saying that it'll lop several noughts off prices, but never gets round to it.

Other information

Republic, capital: Rome. 301,191 square kilometres (116,290 square miles). Population: 57,250,000.

Luxemburg

Luxemburg is a tiny and hilly country in which fairy-tale castles cling to wooded hillsides. It's actually the size of a medium British county, and yet it has full international status.

Language

There are three languages. The first is Luxemburgeois, the other two are French and German. You'll get by if you speak any one of the three, and a lot of people speak English as well.

Accommodation

There are plenty of campsites, ten youth hostels (usually large) which give priority to under-35s, hotels, *auberges* and *pensions*, all at a wide range of prices.

Given the smallness of the place, there's no shortage of accommodation. If you need help, look for the *Syndicat d'Initiative*.

Cycling
There are more minor roads than any tiny country might decently wish for, so make sure you use a map. The main roads are intolerably busy in mid-summer.
    There are a good number of bike shops.

Weather
Much the same as in southern Britain, with the Belgian hills keeping off some of the rain.

Public transport
Trains carry bikes without fuss and cheaply, provided there's room. Buy a ticket and load the bike yourself.

Maps
The Michelin map at 1:200,000 is all you'll need.

Useful addresses
Luxemburg National Tourist Office, 36 Piccadilly, London W1V 9PA (01–434 2800).
Union Luxemburgeoise de Cyclotourism, 39 rue de l'Étoile, 57190 Florange.

Currency
The Luxemburg franc, which is equal to the Belgian franc, which is also legal tender. Perversely, you can't spend Luxemburgeois money in Belgium.

Other information
Grand Duchy, capital: Luxemburg. 2,587 square kilometres (999 square miles). Population: 400,000.

The Netherlands

The Netherlands is a delightful country, although it's hard to work out why. It's not at all the cyclists' paradise that common legend paints it to be. Nor is it especially attractive. In fact, there are so many Dutchmen fighting for so little space that the towns are ceaseless blocks of apartments and housing estates (all with drawn net curtains and pot plants), and the countryside is so cluttered that you can see one village from the next.

The beauty, such as it is, is man-made – the windmills, old castles, merchants' houses and canals. The countryside is totally flat except in the south-eastern province Limburg, which sticks like a panhandle into the junction of West Germany, Belgium and France. And there, on the Netherlands' highest hill, 321 metres up, you can gaze into four countries.

None of the Netherlands is spectacular, but it exudes an organized and well-mannered charm. The midlands – Rotterdam, Amsterdam, The Hague – are too crowded for worthwhile pleasure cycling (although a bike is often most convenient) but the countryside in the eastern half of Nord-Brabant and in Overijssel holds the greatest pleasures.

The Dutch talk of living above, between and below the rivers – the two great rivers, the Maas and the Waal that divide the Netherlands across the middle. The midlanders are the most efficient, Germanic and, according to the other Dutch, the most unfriendly and neurotic. Those in the north are the most relaxed and, by repute, the most stupid. They are much more agricultural and, being remote from the rest of the country, good targets for abuse. Below the rivers, the people are shorter, darker and more likely to be Roman Catholic. They consider themselves fun-loving, but the rest of the Netherlands views them as being almost Belgian, which to a Dutchman is not flattery. These are distinctions much more obvious to a native than a visitor, by the way.

Language

There are two official languages in the Netherlands – Dutch and Frisian. Both are actually quite similar to English, Frisian even more than Dutch, but you'd never know it from seeing them written or even spoken. Fortunately, there's scarcely a soul in the Netherlands who doesn't speak English somewhere in the range of adequate to fluent.

Frisian is spoken only in the north-western province of Vriesland and is entirely incomprehensible even to Dutch-speakers.

Official Dutch is called 'ABN' (not to be confused with ABN, which is a big bank chain) and you hear it on the radio. It's only spoken habitually in the town of Haarlem, west of Amsterdam, and everyone else speaks both with an accent and with a dialect. If you learn a little Dutch, don't fret too much that you can't follow conversations in a bar; the Dutch speak dialect whenever they can.

Some people reckon that they can pin-point the individual villages from which strangers come so much does accent and dialect change. The impact of dialect and the late standardization of written Dutch (after the war) means several places have different names and a few villages have names known only to locals. St Willebrord, near Roosendaal, for example, is only ever called ' 't Heike'.

Since we also anglicize more than a few names, it's worth knowing the main differences so that you can follow a map. The principal ones are:

In English	In Dutch
Flushing	Vlissingen
Den Bosch	's-Hertogenbosch *or* Den Bosch
Hook of Holland	Hoek van Holland
The Hague	Den Haag *or* 's-Gravenhage
Zuiderzee	Ijsselmeer

Unbelievably, Dutch is actually very close to English. Once you peel away the innumerable word prefixes and endings (one word in five starts with or involves the letters *ge*), you're left with something not unlike old English.

Accommodation

There is not, in my experience, any such thing as a cheap hotel room in the Netherlands. The pressure on land, especially in the west midlands, makes building prices astronomical. Many Dutchmen have no hope of ever buying their own homes, which means that hotels aren't cheap to run or inexpensive to stay in. Having said that, family-run hotels can be reasonable, at least, but remember that you pay per person and not by the room.

Room prices have to be hung in the reception area and, as elsewhere in the Netherlands, have to be the final price. In other words, you won't (or shouldn't be) stung for extras. This applies to other things also and means that you don't even have to tip a Dutch taxi driver, since his tip is already reckoned in the fare.

Luckily, no country in the world is as organized for the benefit of tourists. Every town has a branch of the VVV (*Vereniging voor Vreemdelingsverkeer*), pronounced and always referred to as the fay-fay-fay. The best place to start looking is the railway station because, if it's not located there, the chances are that it's nearby. The VVV, for a few guilders, will hunt the town ceaselessly to find you a hotel room at the price you want. It'll also hand you leaflets, street maps and, if they exist, invaluable specialist cycling maps of the immediate area. The VVV will also point you towards the nearest campsite (*kampeerterrein* or *kampeerplaats*) or youth hostel (*jeugdherberg*).

There are a large number of campsites in the Netherlands, although the greatest concentration is along the coast, especially on the most popular coast to the west of the midlands towns. This means that they can be large and, on warm days, extremely busy. That stretch of coast is not only the best the Dutch have but also the most accessible for millions of Germans.

Wild camping is just about impossible in the Netherlands, but there's a compromise offered by the Bosbeheer, the equivalent of our Forestry Commission. There, in a few places, you'll find specifically quiet campsites. The VVV will give you details. You'll need a camping carnet, which you can obtain from the CTC or the motoring organizations. You can also get a list of campsites specifically for cyclists from an organization called Stichting Gastvrije Fiets-campings. I've never seen one of these sites, or stayed on one, so I can't comment, but the idea sounds wonderful. The address is: Postbus 27, 4493 ZG Kamperland.

There are close on sixty youth hostels, again mainly along the coast and on the north-western islands. They are large by British standards and, like British and German hostels, over-used by school parties. They are hospitable and comfortable, though, and often have a small bar.

If you plan to stay in one place for some time, write to the VVV in the nearest town (just VVV, Amersfoort, or wherever, is enough of an address) and ask about holiday bungalows. They go by different names according to the operators, and the standards vary, but they're cheaper than staying in a hotel and more comfortable than camping.

Cycling

Dutch motorists drive very fast, especially in Belgium, which makes the Belgians hopping mad. But they're also very considerate to cyclists, not least because nearly everybody in the Netherlands rides a bike at some time.

Road surfaces are fair to good. There are very few stretches of cobbles these days (the Dutch, with morbid humour, call cobbles *kinderkopjes*, which means children's heads) but most town and village centres are paved with small tiles called *klinkers*. They're about the same size as floor tiles and laid herring-bone fashion. In theory they should do no more than ripple your front wheel and tingle your wrists. In practice they dip and dive at crazy angles and shake you about a lot. Not for nothing do the Dutch ride super-soggy, all-absorbing black roadsters.

Cycle paths (*fietspad*) are numerous and compulsory. They usually follow main roads, although in the country they can be a lane of the road marked by a broad white line. The conventional blue circular signs are rarely put up without some incomprehensible official notices bolted to them. These signs never refer to you, so don't worry about them.

The big difference from Britain is that paths share the priority of the road that they parallel. So when the main road has priority over side roads, so will you. Motorists should – and do – give you priority whether they're coming from your right or turning off the main road from your left. This takes some getting used to.

The drawback is that cycle paths are also used by little motorbikes called *brommers* or *bromfietsen*, which can apparently be ridden only with the feet hitched up by the petrol tank and the incessant bleeping of an irritating electric buzzer. The only speed they go at is flat-out. The Dutch call them *brommers* because that is the sound they make. It is, though, a nasal, soprano *brom* with the whine of a trapped bluebottle.

Cycle paths have their own signposting. The main traffic has blue signs, *you* have white signs at waist-height with red lettering and a little red bicycle. These are a mixed blessing. At best, they take you away from the busiest areas of town and out to wherever you want to go. At worst, though, the signposting is eccentric and erratic. It is wise to always use a map as well.

There are cross-country paths in some areas. These are blissful, but by no means as frequent as people would have you believe. They're not shown on the Michelin maps and you have to look out for little, white, concrete toadstools with directions on them.

Always ask Dutchmen why even quite minor roads are marked at 100-metre intervals by green plates showing the distance (from where? to where?). Few people know, nobody ever seems to have used them, but they're there.

There are several roads in the Netherlands on which you can't ride. You can't use the motorways (*snelwegen*) and A roads. The usual sign is a large oblong with a picture of a car on it. But not all exclusions apply to cyclists. Look for the words *behalve* or, more usually, *uitgezonderd*, which both mean 'except'. If the sign includes the words *fietsen* or *(brom)fietsen*, it means you're not included in the ban.

Other seemingly meaningless road signs are:

Doorgand verkeer	Through traffic
Andere richtingen	Other directions
Woonerf	A housing area designed to hinder cars but allow cyclists and playing children

There are a number of signposted cycling and motoring routes in the Netherlands. You can get details, some with descriptions of the countryside as well as road directions, from the ANWB (see the address list).

There are plenty of bike shops, some general, some specialist. They're called *fietsenwinkels* and pronounced *feets'n'vinkles*, a memorable name. You'll have trouble getting a 27-inch tyre.

As you ride around the Netherlands, marvel at the lengths to which councils will go to cram the names and qualifications of local bigwigs into road signs: Dr Johannes Marinus van Hooydonkstraat, for example. It must cost a fortune in taxes for the extra lengths of street name.

Weather

Dutch weather is akin to southern British, but a little colder in winter (especially inland) and a few degrees warmer in summer. It is, though, almost invariably windy, with nothing to stop the gales coming off the North Sea. Expect some mist in the mornings, clearing quickly, and rainy intervals, especially in December.

Public transport

A good rail network with clean, punctual and down-to-earth trains which often take bikes. Further details appear earlier, on page 80. You buy a bike ticket at the station and load the bike yourself.

The big attraction of the rail service is that NS (the railway company) often have bargain return fares. The return fare, for example, can be only a guilder more than the single. And note that when you travel from Britain, the fare to the Netherlands is the same whichever station you get out at, whether it's the first stop beyond Hoek van Holland or the furthest-flung station in Friesland.

There's an internal air service but distances are so short that they're not worth considering unless you're combining them with a trip from outside the country.

Maps

The best everyday maps are the Michelin 1:200,000, which cover the whole country in four sheets. It's safe to ride on any minor road that Michelin shows, unlike in neighbouring Belgium. They don't show cycle paths, though.

For details like that you need the wonderful ANWB *Toeristenkaart* at 1:100,000. It shows not only cycle paths but the roads on which you *can't* ride: very useful.

Useful addresses

Netherlands Tourist Office, 25–28 Buckingham Gate, London SW1E 6LD
    (01–630 0451).
ANWB, Wassenaarseweg 220, 2596 EC The Hague.
Nederlandse Rijwiel Toer Unie (the cycle-touring organization), Vendelier 27, PB
    326, 3900 Veenendaal.
Stichting Fiets (a trade group which campaigns for cyclists and which will send
    you maps and information, much of it in Dutch), Europaplein 2, 1078 GZ
    Amsterdam.
Nederlandse Spoorwegen (the railway company, whose leaflets on bikes are in
    Dutch but whose officials can be persuaded to answer letters in English),
    Moreelspark 1, Utrecht.

Currency

The guilder, written locally as *gulden* but pronounced much the same since the final 'n' is silent in conventional Dutch. It's abbreviated as *f* or *fl*, from the days when a guilder was a florin.

There are 100 cents to a guilder.

Other information

Kingdom, principal city: Amsterdam, seat of government: The Hague. 41,160 square kilometres (15,892 square miles). Population: 14,250,000.

Norway

Don't head for Norway unless you're mentally tough and physically self-sufficient. It's a grand country but one which towers over the individual. It's hilly, mountainous indeed, often wet and cold, and roads can deteriorate as they steepen.

It's certainly not for beginners. Yet no country, with the possible exception of Iceland, offers the same thrill. Places are a long way apart since the entire population is less than London's. And frankly, so far as I can see, the entire population is also rather sombre and reserved, not unfriendly but nevertheless morose. It must be all that walking about on wet streets.

Perhaps it's the wet streets too, that account for the Norwegian habit of taking off shoes when visiting somebody else's house.

Norway is not a cheap place.

Language

Norwegian, although nearly everybody speaks English and Swedish as well.

Accommodation

Look for the TTK in each town for local information. There are campsites in the south, and youth hostels, excellent ones, going far enough north for the weather to start closing in. Wild camping is obviously possible in such an unpopulated country but you mustn't pitch near a house or stay for more than two days.

Hotels are good but costly. Look instead for *pensjonats*, *hospits* and *gjestgjiveries*, which are guest houses. If you don't see those signs, look for *rom* or *husrom*.

Mountain huts (*hytter*) are available further north and you can get information before you leave, from the national tourist office.

Cycling

There's no such thing as a busy road in Norway unless it's directly leading to Oslo. Road surfaces get worse as you head north. At first it's the minor roads that lose their surface, then the main roads as well. They become mucky in the wet and dusty in the dry.

Expect some long climbs but only occasionally very steep ones; Norwegian road engineers are enthusiastic about digging tunnels. That's the good news; the bad news is that the tunnels are long and pitch black. They also drip icy water. Worse, the tunnel walls are jagged and the tunnels bend in the middle. You need good lights, no oncoming traffic to dazzle you, total concentration and a lot of courage.

Don't rely on bike shops. They exist in towns, but where are the towns?

Off-road riding? Perfect. And what's more, you can go wherever you wish with just the most obvious exceptions.

Weather

Winter makes much of upland Norway impassable. In the summer the snow turns to rain, but late summer can be surprisingly mild, especially to the west, thanks to the sea. Summers are brief but the days very long.

Public transport

There are only main train lines and no branches, and the trains go about as fast as you'd expect in a mountainous land. They're also quite costly.

You can, in principle, take your bike by train provided you buy a ticket, which for short journeys works out very expensive. There are, though, difficult exclusions and it's essential to ring the station.

You can get a long way fast or get to out-of-the-way places by using ferries.

Maps

Use the Cappelen 1:325,000 or 400,000.

Useful addresses

Norwegian Tourist Office, 5–11 Lower Regent Street, London SW1 (01–839 6255).

Currency

The krone, made up of 100 öre.

Other information

Kingdom, capital: Oslo. 323,895 square kilometres (125,057 square miles). Population: 4,100,000.

Portugal

A long and dusty country which in spring bursts into the colour of blossom as the fruit trees reach their peak, Portugal is a subtle country rather than a spectacular one. You can lose yourself happily along bumpy, winding back lanes that run through small farms where chickens run loose on the road.

Portugal's big earner is tourism, which is crammed into a concrete jungle along the Algarve and the south-western coast. The Algarve in a few years will be as beyond recovery as the worst of the Spanish costas, the Portuguese priding themselves that at least they're doing it with large and up-market holiday villages rather than featureless hotel blocks. All the same, the coastal strip offers you very little except a sunny beach and an alternative to cycling.

The holiday industry does mean good communications with Britain, though, and there are some remarkable bargains if you're prepared to fly out in the spring or late winter. Because the climate is so equable, and because the best scenery comes before the hottest sun, this can be a bonus.

Portugal is Britain's oldest ally, a fact with which the Portuguese are more familiar than the British. Since Portugal hasn't seen the worst of the costa yobbery, this alliance is likely to survive.

Language

Very few people speak English away from the southern coast, but you might be able to make yourself understood in Spanish (which is quite a different language but at least looks similar when it's written down).

Accommodation

There are only a dozen youth hostels but there are hotels in the towns, usually reasonably priced. Look for the *Turismo* office. Less prestigious accommodation is available in *estalgem* (inns), *pousada* (state inns), and *residencia* (boarding houses).

Cycling

The road from Faro airport is appalling and busy at every hour of the day. Apart from that one, the roads are just about empty. On the other hand, they're also pretty poor. The road surface can vary from kilometre to kilometre, from immaculate to bone-jarring. Unlike most southern countries, the roads get worse as you go north. In the northern towns, some streets are scarcely ridable.

The Portuguese drive fast and have very brown left arms, from their habit of sticking them out of open windows. They're safe, though. Don't rely on (or even look for) signposting.

You'll find bike shops in Lisbon and Oporto but almost nowhere else.

Weather

Always warm, sometimes very hot in the extreme south. The wind blows off the sea and drops what moisture it carries in the mountains, where there can be spectacular storms.

Public transport

Railway stations operate at the same gentle pace as the various sidelines. Most trains take bikes, but get to the station with half an hour to spare. You'll need it to cope with the paperwork, which is all in dense Portuguese.

Maps

There aren't enough roads to make a large scale essential, and local maps are often out of date. Use the Michelin 1:500,000, which covers the whole country.

Useful addresses

Portuguese Tourist Office, 1–5 New Bond Street, London W1Y 0NP (01–493 3873).

Currency

The escudo, written $ and divided into 100 centavos.

Other information

Republic, capital: Lisbon. 91,631 square kilometres (35,379 square miles). Population: 10,000,000.

Spain

A surprisingly and impressively empty country. Not for nothing do the Spanish tourist people repeatedly advertise for you to discover the 'real', inland Spain. When you're there, it goes on for ever.

The countryside varies, although it's never at all subtle. You're either in fertile patches or huge barren stretches that you feel you've seen in a dozen

cowboy films – and you probably have. There are few big towns. Instead, inland
Spain has small villages, some of which are poor in the extreme. Because
they're so far apart, it would be wise to carry extra water.

Whatever you do, don't forget how enormous Spain is – or under-estimate
how long it will take you to ride across it or even part of it. And remember, that
although there are topless girls on the beaches, inland Spain is still reserved.
Don't wear shorts in churches, for example.

Language

Spanish, although the people just south of the Pyrenees often speak French.
You can get a long way in *written* Spanish if you apply English and your
knowledge of French with dollops of guesswork and commonsense. It doesn't
always work, though. Asking at a post office for *timbros* (from the French,
timbre) produced not a postage stamp but a rubber one.

You'll find English is spoken in the tourist areas.

Accommodation

Finding somewhere to stay in Spain is not easy. The Spanish have compensated
for all those millions of hotel rooms around the coast by building hardly any
elsewhere. Youth hostels are mainly up in the hills and there are campsites
along the coast but rarely in other places. You're strongly advised, inland, to
camp wild. In fact, with the weather the way it is, you don't actually need a tent.
Many towns have no hotels at all, so, if you find one that has, take whatever it is
you're offered.

Where hotels exist, they're usually signposted or have a metal plate outside.
Look for the letters P (*pensión*), H (*hostale*), HsR (*hostale-residencia*) and CH
(*casa de huéspedes*). On the off-chance that there is one, look for a *Turismo*
plaque, which denotes the *Oficina de Informacíon y Turismo*.

The universal sign-language of looking lost and placing two hands on the
side of your tilted head will get you far – unless you do it to a woman, when it
might well be misunderstood.

If you camp wild, make this a general rule: never camp within several
hundred metres of anything at all. Keep away from houses, roads, streams,
factories, air bases . . . anything. The Spanish allow wild camping only on these
conditions.

Cycling

The roads on the coast, especially within 20 miles of an airport, are suicidal.
Some have a European reputation for summer carnage. Elsewhere the roads are
quiet. The cross-country roads will be surfaced, although they get worse as you
go south, but the byways are just as you see in cowboy films. Expect Wells
Fargo and dust clouds any minute.

The holiday coast is no longer worth considering. Even the king publicly regretted the kind of clientele his country's fringes were attracting. To cater for them, minute fishing villages have been transformed into ugly, sprawling cities of tower blocks and Queen Victoria pubs. Where the coast goes upmarket, the tower blocks and discos give way to holiday condominiums, time-share apartments and second-home villas (Spanish for bungalows).

Another country for self-sufficiency. Bike shops are unknown outside the towns. Drivers are seemingly taught to approach cyclists as quietly as possible and then blast their horns before accelerating past.

Weather

Expect some rain all year round along the northern coast, but otherwise it's warm everywhere. Mid-summer is impossibly hot, especially since water is short inland.

Public transport

There are trains in Spain and they do, sometimes, carry bikes. Mainly, though, it would be every bit as quick to cycle. If you really break down, take a train no further than the nearest city that has an airport. Then use one of the internal air services to get you somewhere worthwhile.

Maps

The Michelin 1:1,000,000 is just about good enough. It shows the kind of road surface, although the smallest tracks are omitted.

Useful addresses

Spanish National Tourist Office, 57–58 St James's Street, London SW1A 1LD (01–499 0901).
Gibraltar Tourist Office, 179 Strand, London WC2R 1EH (01–836 0777).
ANCE (Spanish campsite organization), Gran Via 88 10–8, Madrid 28013.
REAJ (Spanish YHA), José Ortega y Gasset 71, 28006 Madrid.

Currency

The peseta, which should be too small to be divided any further. It is, though. There are 100 céntimos.

Other information

Kingdom, capital: Madrid. 504,879 square kilometres (194,935 square miles). Population: 38,000,000.

Sweden

Much of what applied to the geography of Norway applies also to Sweden, although on a gentler scale. The south of the country is actually quite easygoing, especially in contrast to the uplands.

From there going northwards, of course, the riding gets harder and bleaker the further you go. By the time you get north of the capital, Stockholm, you realize that you're in a hard, under-populated country. By the time you reach Lapland, you really are in remote, savage country and life is an adventure. This far north isn't for the weak and wary. The rest of Sweden, though, is by no means as mountainous as neighbouring Norway.

The drawback of Sweden is its cost. Nothing in Sweden is cheap, including the food. This must be due to one of those quirks of international money exchanges, keeping the krona especially high and prices to outsiders, therefore, breathtaking. I say this because the Swedes themselves are well off and have a high standard of living. If it seemed as expensive to them as it does to us, that wouldn't be possible.

Language
Swedish, which many see as the 'standard' Scandinavian language. English is widely spoken.

Accommodation
Most of the accommodation – including 300 youth hostels and 750 campsites – is in the south, which is where the people are. The hostels are not large by European standards, well run and largely seasonal. They also suffer the curse of the school party, a fact not alleviated by their relative smallness.

Further north, the choice is either to camp – there is endless wild camping and a legal right to be on open country – or use mountain lodges run by the Swedish Touring Club, which you have to join. The tourist office will have details.

On the outskirts of towns you might see houses advertising a room (*rum*) for hire. Breakfast isn't always provided.

Cycling
The main roads in the south are busy – Sweden has a lot of heavy industry – mostly with Volvo and Saab cars and aircraft. Further north the roads are quieter and even further north they're silent.

All main roads are surfaced but the secondary roads aren't. They're soggy in winter and dusty in the summer. You'll need good tyres. It might even be worth taking a spare because bike shops are scarce outside the towns.

Weather

Summer is short – June, July and August, south of Stockholm – but it rarely rains anywhere. May and June are the prettiest months; August is fine but, as in France, it's when the whole population goes on holiday and everywhere outside the holiday areas shuts down.

Public transport

You can take your bike on the train, but not necessarily on the same one as yourself. It'll follow you a day or two days afterwards. The flat fee makes it expensive for a short journey, a bargain for a long one.

There's also an internal air network.

Maps

Not easy to get in a large scale. Two sheets of the G.I.A. series cover the country at 1:1,000,000 but a lot of height information is missing, so it pays to be cautious and to consult guide books before you go.

Useful addresses

Swedish Tourist Board, 3 Cork Street, London W1X 1HA (01–437 5816).
Cykelfrämjandet (the Swedish CTC), Stora Nygatan 41–43, 103 12 Stockholm.
Svenska Cykelsällskapet (another general cycling body), Box 6006, 164 06 Kista.

Currency

The krona, written *kr.*

Other information

Kingdom, capital: Stockholm. 449,792 square kilometres (15,941 square miles). Population: 6,500,000.

Switzerland

Another expensive and arduous country, Switzerland can be busy for much of the year, even though the government has gone to a lot of trouble to stop motorists using it as a short cut to France. A good country for challenging yourself on mountain passes, of which there are more than a few. The most popular, though, are now too heavily used to be enjoyable. To find a quieter col means coping with bad surfaces, frequent hairpins and unfenced, sheer drops.

Language

French, German, Italian and Romainsch. The last is indecipherable, the others heavily accented. Many people speak more than one and quite a few can manage English as well.

Accommodation

Details are very similar to those in neighbouring Germany, except the hotels are dearer and classier. Wild camping is easy.

Cycling

Road surfaces range from excellent (the main roads) to cobbled (parts of town centres). Generally they're fine, though, but busy on the through routes, including the main mountain passes. Beware trams in the lowlands and post buses (which have priority over everything and insist on taking it) in the highlands.

Tunnels through the mountains are scary, dark and wet.

Weather

The weather is quite unpredictable and depends entirely on the mountains, the valleys and the wind direction.

Public transport

All but the inter-city expresses take bikes, as do the post buses if they've got room.

Maps

The Michelin 1:200,000 series is fine. It covers the whole country in four sheets.

Currency

The Swiss franc, one of the securest and most expensive currencies in the world. It's divided into 100 centimes.

Other information

Confederated republic, capital: Berne. 41,288 square kilometres (15,941 square miles). Population: 6,750,000.

III. Your Bicycle

10. Nuts and Bolts

By now, of course, you may very well be thinking you could do with a new bicycle. Good for you. After all, a better bike has much the same effect as a better pair of shoes: it's more comfortable, it helps you ride further or faster and more enjoyably. It's always puzzled me that folk who won't drive round in a twenty-year-old car insist on riding a bike that's even older. Times have changed for the bicycle as well, and if you haven't had a close look at what's around these days, I think you'll be surprised – not least at the way very complicated alloys have replaced steel and at the arrival of whizzo technology like click-stop gearing.

BIKE SHOPS

What you need first is a good bike shop. It might mean travelling several miles, but you'll not regret it. There'll be a decent shop no more than 15 miles away (unless you live in the Highlands) and probably very much nearer. There are a lot of good shops and no list can be conclusive, but some of the nationally-known ones are as follows.

SOUTH

Ken Bird, 35–37 High Street, Green Street Green, Orpington, Kent (0689–537476).
Dees, 39 Hill Avenue, Amersham (02043–7165).
Ealing, 16 Bond Street, London W4 (01–567 3557).
F. W. Evans, 48 Richmond Road, Kingston, Surrey (01–549 2559) and 77–79 The Cut, London SE1 (01–928 4785).
Freewheel, 275 West End, London NW6 (01–794 4133).
Get On Your Bike, 5 Bridge Street, Godalming, Surrey GU7 1HY (04868–20055).
Ben Hayward, 69 Trumpington Street, Cambridge (0223–352294).
Hetchins, 117 Hamstel Road, Southend (0702–466819).
London Bridge, 41 Railway Approach, London SE1 9SS (01–403 1690).
C. B. Ransom, 86 Victoria Road, Alton, Hants (0420–82867).
Richmond Cycles, 36 Hill Street, Richmond, Surrey (01–940 6961).
W. F. Holdsworth, Lower Richmond Road, Putney (01–785 6308).

J. D. Whisker, 684a Goffs Lane, Goffs Oak, Herts (070787–5448) and
   80 Willesden Lane, Kilburn, London NW6 (01–624 6375).
Geoff Wiles, 47 Cuxton Road, Strood, Kent (0634–722587/727416).
Youngs, 286–290 Lee High Road, Lewisham (01–852 6880/1848).

EAST MIDLANDS

Beacon Cycles, 88 Derby Road, Loughborough (0509–215448).
George Halls, 12 Northampton Road, Market Harborough (0858–65507).
Julies, 212–216 Clarendon Park Road, Leicester (0533–707936).
Mercian, 7 Shardlow Road, Alvaston, Derby (0332–752468).
Reynolds Cycles, Wellingborough Road, Northampton (0604–30586).
Terry Wright, 39 Bridge Street, Deeping St James, Lincs (0778–344051).

WEST MIDLANDS

John Atkins Cycles, 140 Far Gosford Street, Coventry (0203–22997).
Bearwood Cycles, 428–432 Bearwood Road, Smethwick, Warley, Birmingham
   B66 4EY (021–429 2199).

EAST ANGLIA

Buckley-Saxon, St James St, Castle Hedingham, Essex (0787–61755).
Frank Kirby, 5 St Benedicts Street, Norwich (0603–627444).
Madgett, Wills Yard, Chapel Street, Diss, Norfolk (0379–2735).

WEST

Avon Valley Cyclery, 37–38 Dorchester Street, Bath (0225–61880).
Fred Baker, 144 Cheltenham Road, Bristol BS6 5RL (0272–249610).
G and A Gray, 17 Pickwick Road, Corsham, Wilts (0249–713045).
Colin Lewis, Paignton, Devon (0803–553095).
Pedersen Cycles, 21 Parsonage Street, Dursley, Glos (0453–46755).

WALES

Deeside Cycles, 5 Chester Road East, Shotton, Clwyd (0244–822321).

NORTH WEST

Bicycle Doctor, 68 Dickenson Road, Rusholme, Manchester (061–224 1303).
Harry Hall, Cathedral Square, Manchester (061–832 1369).
Lakeland, 3 Whin Drive, Bolton-le-Sands, Carnforth (0524–735465).
Pedal Power, Waddington Road, Clitheroe, Lancs (0200–22066).

NORTH EAST

Colin Armstrong, 22 Princes Street, Middlesbrough (0642–244027).
Bentley Cycles, 31–33 Knowle Terrace, Leeds LS4 2PA (0532–783505).
Bob Jackson, 148 Harehills Lane, Leeds (0532–493022).
Paul Milnes, 461 Gt Horeton Road, Bradford BD7 3DJ (0274–576197).
Settle Cycles, Duke Street, Settle, N. Yorks BD24 9DJ (07292–2216).
M. Steel, 2 Station Road, South Gosforth, Newcastle upon Tyne (091–285
    1251).
Two Wheels Good, 35 Call Lane, Leeds LS1 7BT (0532–456867).
Universal, 122 Manor Road, Maltby, Rotherham, S. Yorks (0709–813089).

SCOTLAND

Sandy Gilchrist, 1 Cadzow Place, Abbeyhill, Edinburgh (031–652 1760).
Robin Williamson, 26 Hamilton Place, Stockbridge, Edinburgh EH3 5AU (031–
    225 3286).

IRELAND

Dave Kane, 309 Upper Newtownards Road, Ballyhackamore, Belfast (0232–
    653139).

There are a fair number of advertisements every other month in the pages of
Cycletouring, and a great number (aimed principally at racing cyclists but not
totally excluding leisure riders) in each week's *Cycling Weekly* (9–13 Ewell
Road, Cheam, Surrey SM1 4QQ; 01–661 4351 and 4359). *Cycling Weekly* has,
in Peter Knottley, one of the most experienced and genial touring advisers that
any magazine could wish. A further reasonable if rather more expensive source
of advertisements are the weekly magazines like *Bicycle* and *Winning*, which
you'll find at the bigger newsagents. *Cycling World* has very few advertisements
but it does have the homely feel of a club magazine and a good readers' advice
service. The address is Stone Publications, 2a Station Road, Sidcup, Kent. It
appears monthly.

Perils for the Unwary

A bicycle is a bicycle is a bicycle, you may think. But you'd be wrong. If you
wanted to, you could go straight out and be guided by price alone. After all,
there are more apparent bargains now than at any time. You're being wooed by
ingenious factories, some building up to a standard, others making down to a
price. But the golden rule is that you get what you pay for. Rogues and
charlatans apart – and there aren't too many of those in the cycling world – the
noughts in the price are a good guide to quality.

Low prices can mean non-standard parts, unavailable spares and shoddy engineering. It gets worse when these bargains are sold by garages feeling the pinch of higher petrol prices, and by department stores and supermarkets. These places even sell well-known makes – especially after a recent court case – often for less than the standard price. But try taking the bike back for a service or advice once you've parted with your money. Specialist bike shops, where the owner's got oily hands, may charge more, but the experience, service and advice are included. Just try asking a supermarket to replace a cotter pin on a Saturday afternoon . . .

Once you cross the shop threshold, there are bikes of all kinds. There's everything from the lofty and tireless black roadsters beloved of the Dutch to the very expensive, super-lightweight competition machines on which Greg LeMond and Sean Kelly ride the Tour de France and world championship.

Fortunately, you can break up this bewildering range into classes.

WHICH BIKE?

The plodder

The round-the-village plodder guarantees dependence and stubborn reliability. Its origins are in the all-black push-bike which did so much to help the motor car. Some of those which are still on the road saw service in the First World War. They and their progeny have straight or sit-up-and-beg handlebars, rod brakes, single gears (one-speed freewheel) and sturdy tyres on wheels held apart by a no-nonsense frame.

They are just about unbreakable. They are nearly always painted black. They occasionally have three-speed gears. In some parts, they carry village postmen on country tracks, midwives on errands, policemen on their rounds. In the Netherlands, where there are more bicycles than Dutchmen, ardent young men carry their girlfriends above the back wheel. Go to the East and the same heavy bikes pull rickshaws and other trailers, some loaded to breathtaking weight. They're the bicycles that go to war: the 26th Middlesex (Cyclist) Volunteer Rifle Corps in 1888, for example, and 14 cyclists' battalions in the First World War. The bicycle, said H. G. Wells, who was fond of them, 'may be destined to be the dominant arm in the European warfare of the future'. The North Vietnamese used them to carry supplies in their troubles with the Americans.

Verdict: Fine for riding down to the library. Otherwise much too heavy and miserable.

The sports

Next up the list is the sports machine, with lighter equipment, a mattress saddle, multiple gearing and straight or slightly rounded handlebars. For short-distance commuting or first trips into the countryside, there's nothing better.

The comfortable, relaxed riding position demands no special clothing; light-weights, by contrast, can't be comfortably ridden without a tracksuit and perhaps cycling shoes.

Sports bikes' pedals are rubber blocks, perfect for conventional shoes in the dry, and the top of the chain is enclosed. That means you can wear normal trousers without trouser clips. The sports bike is light but not featherweight. Its frame is lively without being frisky, and its equipment draws the line between solid monotony and the sophistication which makes cycling a dream achieved only by constant tinkering.

Verdict: A good bike for rides of up to, say, ten miles. Good for its price, dependable, unexciting. But it wastes a little energy and the one riding position can be monotonous if relaxed.

The small-wheeler

The sports machine has developed sideways into the small-wheeled shopper, although the shopper's true origins lie in a nifty small-wheeler produced by Alex Moulton during the swinging sixties. Moulton, a brain in the motor design industry, had thought about bumps and jolts on bad roads, and about the impracticalities of large wheels. His problem was to reduce the size of the wheels, to produce a bike which would have more space for luggage, without making a bumpier ride. Shorter spokes bend less and soak up fewer road bumps, sending them to the rider.

The Americans, who had long favoured small wheels, compromised by producing huge, spongy tyres with little pressure to keep them in shape. The Americans, though, saw bicycles as children's pavement toys to be ridden only a few hundred yards at a time, so the energy-sapping, super-sog, balloon tyres were no problem.

Moulton wanted a bike on which to explore the world. He wanted it to ride 150 miles a day, perhaps with touring luggage, and he didn't want to do it against the resistance of soggy tyres. He wanted 16-inch wheels. His invention in 1962 was bicycle suspension. Others had done it before, of course, but Moulton got it just about right. He put sprung suspension immediately above the front forks and had a heavily-damped pivot between the bottom bracket and the chainstays. There were no rear forks.

Raleigh took over production in 1967. By that time it was obvious that the suspension was an extra source of wear and tear, and they abandoned it. Within ten years the only Moulton you could buy was a children's version. Moulton, after a long silence, heavily modified his design and it's now back in much smaller and rather more expensive production. An owners' club provides spares and companionship to those who cling to the 20-year-old original.

The poor substitute was the shopper. Gone was the suspension, gone was the quality of engineering. Instead, a wheel larger than Moulton's but smaller than normal and a tyre which was as soft as the makers dared. Where Moulton had found space for the biggest bags – even travellers who spent a month camping in Iceland had difficulty filling them – the shoppers had bags just big enough to carry a moderate amount of shopping.

Despite all this, they haven't failed. The price stayed low and they have sold. But they're for short trips to a shopping centre and back. The little rigid wheels make it hard work, and so does the cramped position. I could tolerate buying things by shopper – I couldn't imagine wanting to see the world from one.

Verdict: Avoid anything with less than a 26-inch wheel unless it's a child's bike or a new Moulton. The older style of Moultons are now two decades old and spares may prove difficult to obtain. The new Moultons aren't cheap but very few people switch back to conventional bikes once they've tried one. They're superb for travel with luggage.

The lightweight

This lightweight is the next step up the ladder. It's frisky. It's easy to ride. It's comfortable enough to take you right through the night and it's useful enough to take you to work and back.

Now, it's common to think that anything with dropped handlebars is a racer. It rarely is. The tyres on my lightweight may be narrow and they're certainly pumped harder than normal – 90 lb a square inch – but they're not by any means as light or zippy as a racing bike's. I take my tyres off with levers and discover an inner tube. The racing man rips his glued-on tyres off a half-moon, shallow rim and then faces a long job unstitching a cotton tube to get to the inner tube that held the air.

Everything else may be superficially similar – the dropped handlebars, the gears and the apparently hard, narrow saddle. My bike, though, with its mudguards and its lights, is a lightweight; the other is a racer. It's like the difference between a sports car and a racing car.

It's rare to find open-frame 'women's bikes' at this level. Lightweight or racer, the one pattern is a diamond or man's frame. Women ride in tracksuits, trousers or shorts. The diamond frame is, anyway, stronger and lighter than the 'open' frame with its twin down-tubes or the 'mixte' frame with its compromise.

These light bikes also have derailleur gears as standard, often with up to fifteen gears but more usually with ten or twelve. You get the variations by fitting five or six differently-sized sprockets to the rear wheel and heaving the chain from one to the other with a collapsible parallelogram. Mechanically, the system makes engineers wince. Everything is wrong. The chain is pushed across only centimetres from the sprocket in use. It is bent to grind from one set of teeth to another. And in all but one speed, it's running around a horizontal curve, with added wear and friction. Nevertheless, anything intended to replace it has been dearer, heavier or less versatile.

Derailleur gears are almost infinitely variable by replacing the rear sprockets with others of a different size. They can be doubled or even trebled by fitting second and third chainrings between the pedals, like an overdrive. And what's more, as the years pass, they get better and, in real terms, cheaper and cheaper.

Verdict: The lightweight is perfect for rides of ten miles or more. It offers mechanical efficiency, a lively but not difficult ride, and good value for money (although it's relatively expensive). On the other hand, the riding position can make it difficult to ride in conventional clothes, and town shoes don't fit the pedals easily. Highly recommended for longer rides.

Mountain bikes

The mountain bike is a trendy version of the sports machine. It keeps the basic geometry, but the wheels are wider and have heavy, sometimes knobbled tyres. Handlebars are straight and wide. Mudguards are rare.

The mountain bike – sometimes called an all-terrain bike – was born in America where, in much of the countryside, lanes are restricted to single tracks running up into the hills for the benefit of hunters. They peter out at the top and all you have is the option of riding back down again. Soon this developed into a game of its own, with enthusiasts loading several bikes into the back of a pick-up truck, driving high into the hills and then descending at high speed. The one non-combatant drove the empty truck back down again to pick up the wreckage.

The beaten-up bikes soon evolved into something rather more snazzy, though. The old steel wheels and spongy tyres gave way to wider alloy rims and heavily patterned tyres with high pressures. High-quality equipment became fashionable; in many cases it was every bit as good, and expensive, as the gear fitted to pure racing bikes. Special frames were made with wide clearances to stop mud clogging the wheels; wide handlebars became standard for precision control.

Before long, as these things do, the mountain bike became not just the preserve of cross-country riders but of anyone who fancied something fashionable. As a result, in the late eighties they were the biggest-selling of all adult bikes, even in areas like East Anglia which aren't noted for their mountains. They're also the standard mount of cycle messengers in London, where hills are infrequent but potholes are depressingly common.

Mountain bikes don't make good touring bikes because there's no provision for luggage or for staying dry in the rain. That, of course, is part of the macho image. On the other hand, they're comfortable to ride and the quality of the equipment is much higher than on standard sports machines. Because so many people have bought them to use not on mud but on tarmac, a curious mutation has begun in which so-called mountain bikes are now available with slick tyres.

Verdict: Great fun bikes, if expensive considering the alternative. Might yet challenge the conventional lightweight for rides of up to 25 miles, but the restrictions of the sports bike still apply. There's also the inappropriateness of using heavy, energy-absorbing tyres on the open road. On the other hand, for whooping it up on tracks and cross-country, there's nothing better. There are more and more mountain biking clubs and even an established racing calendar.

The racer

Real racing bikes are rarely seen in bike shops. It's not that they don't exist for the ordinary cyclist, it's more that the tradition has been to buy all the parts separately and assemble them at home. Racing bikes, therefore, are highly individual and almost impossible to buy off the peg.

The main difference from other machines is the fragility of the equipment, and in the type of tyres. Lightness is more important than sheer strength, and since lightness doesn't come cheaply, they're expensive as well.

The tyres are rolled on to a half-moon rim and glued in place. The tyre has to be completely removed and unstitched below the reinforcing strip to be repaired.

Verdict: Racing bikes are the state of the art and can cost as much as a small car. They're perfect for racing but they're also bumpy and twitchy to ride and the tyres are too fragile for everyday use. Naturally, there's no provision for mudguards and luggage. And the gearing, which admittedly can be changed, is too high for leisure riding. Do try riding one some time, though.

11. Bolts and Nuts

If you're buying a new bike, buy either a lightweight or a mountain bike. Personally I would recommend a lightweight because, although you can't treat it quite as harshly over mud and rocks, the chances are that you won't want to. If you don't feel happy with dropped handlebars (and heaven's sake, they're not compulsory) a bike shop will change them to sports-type bars for you.

A good bike has the irony that although it needs to fit like a carpet slipper and be twice as comfortable – because it'll be ridden for hours – it looks like it's been drawn from the cupboards of some medieval torturer. The saddle is rock hard; the pedals are metal with two thin cross-members; the handlebars are relatively low, the saddle high; and the brake levers point straight ahead and (on dropped handlebars) vertically, which looks the most impractical.

SADDLES

Well, the answer is that it all works. The saddle is anything but uncomfortable. It's hard because soft ones absorb energy and produce saddle sores; but it's soft where it matters, and many riders hang on to a favourite leather saddle when they sell the rest of their bike. I say leather, but most are basically plastic. Unica plastic saddles appeared in the 1960s, in lurid salmon and other colours. The purists sneered, but the advantages soon showed. They might never have conformed to an individual backside, but they didn't need thousands of miles to break them in either. They were shiny and slippery, and the old British cyclist Tom Simpson cut his wife's handbag to form a leather covering. So was born the composite saddle, a plastic base and a softer surface with better grip, such as chamois.

There are more designs of saddle now than there have been for many years. There are women's saddles, like the Madison, with a shorter nose and a wider cantle, and even something resembling the old 'anatomical' saddle, completely or partly divided to support the ischial bones.

Recommendation: Buy a modern saddle with light padding but no springs. Leather saddles last longer and ultimately they're more comfortable, but they're heavier, more expensive, need a lot of uncomfortable breaking in and mustn't get wet. Saddles are so personal that there's no true guide.

HANDLEBARS

The handlebars are lower than the saddle because they share bodyweight with the saddle and pedals. The brakes are fitted that way because an experienced rider finds them accessible from all directions and because their hoods take the strain of a body shifted forwards by braking.

Recommendation: Always buy alloy handlebars; the days have long gone when they weren't strong enough. And don't fit alloy handlebars to a steel extension because they react together and crack. Buy dropped handlebars unless you have very small hands (in which case you'll find the brake levers difficult to grasp) or unless you're really convinced you won't get on with them.

PEDALS

The pedals are metal so that they won't slip and because they will be used mainly with specialist shoes which have slotted plates on the soles. The pedals also have toeclips, with leather straps. Racing cyclists and tourists tackling a hill tighten them and trap their feet. They pull the strap with one foot as they push the pedal with the other. Slotted plates pull back at the bottom of the stroke, increasing propulsion dramatically.

Easing the pedals round by flexing the foot is called ankling. Old books go into ankling at length, with diagrams of how to drop the heel at the top of the stroke and raise it at the bottom to overcome top dead centre, or the position in which the cranks are vertical and therefore 'dead'. Since then road surfaces have improved and bikes are brighter, so that many riders now keep their toes tilted a little downwards, except on steep climbs.

Getting your feet into toeclips is easier than it sounds. It's no more than flipping the back of the pedal down with the toe and sliding the foot quickly into the clips. Some pedals have an extension at the back to make this easier. Shoeplates click into position on the back cross-frame, but they're not for novices, particularly once the straps are tightened.

Recommendation: Buy metal pedals unless you know you're only going to wear town shoes. If you plan to wear trainers or specialized cycling shoes, fit toe clips for greater efficiency. Pedal prices vary a great deal. Frankly you won't notice a lot of difference provided they're wide enough and you don't buy at the bottom of the price range.

BRAKES

Lightweights – and true racers – also have better brakes. This is partly because the machines are better and the brakes are made of less spongy metal and better designed, and also because the wheels have alloy rims which work better in both the dry and wet. Chromed steel rims of the 1⅜-inch type are alarmingly inefficient at gripping the brake blocks and many makers are fitting only 1¼-inch alloy rims. At the same time, manufacturers are turning out blocks said to be better in wet weather and with chromed steel rims. One of the best, Matthauser, comes from the United States.

Brakes work with a cable either to the side (side-pull) or to the centre (centre-pull). Side-pull are commoner and lighter, but the cheap ones are difficult to adjust. Centre-pull brakes feel spongier but exert greater pressure (especially when, as with the Mafac Driver, they pivot not from the fork crown but, in effect, upside-down from the forks themselves).

The best makes are Campagnolo (very expensive), Shimano (generally good value and highly efficient, but prone to design changes), Weinmann (best at the top of the range) and Mafac (now hard to get). For all that some people swear by side-pull and others by centre-pull, I doubt more than two out of ten could tell the difference if they had their eyes closed.

Many bikes supplied with dropped handlebars are now fitted with so-called 'safety' brake levers. Extension arms run from the top of the levers and twist and run parallel to the top of the handlebars. The theory is that you're no longer obliged to ride with your hands on the brake hoods. It's also supposed to be simpler, if you have small hands, to apply the brakes. Sadly, this is something of an illusion. What happens in practice is that the leverage is too small to be entirely effective, and the metal from which the brake extensions are made is soft enough to flex as they're applied. In many cases it's possible to pull the lever all the way to the handlebars before the brake is fully applied. Therefore safety levers will check your speed but won't properly stop you. To stop dead, you have to release the safety lever, and therefore the brakes, and make a grab for the brake levers. All that takes time.

Do all you can to buy small levers which you can grasp conventionally. If you can't, shrug and settle for straight handlebars and conventional brake levers instead.

Recommendation: You get precisely what you pay for in brakes, except that Campagnolo and the costliest Shimano brakes are overpriced. Buy the best you can and you'll never regret it.

FRAMES

The more specialized or advanced the bike, the shorter its wheelbase: the nearer the wheels, the more responsive the bike. What scientific basis there is, I don't know, but it's true. At the same time, the angles of the head and seat tubes are increased; if they weren't, the wheels would bump on the frame and the top tube would become impossibly short.

Frame-builders refer to a bike's geometry in different ways. They may talk of how far the seat pin bolt is behind the bottom bracket, or of the angles of the tubes themselves. The second is common in Britain and the English-speaking world, although the first, the Continental explanation, gives a better idea of what all this is about.

The old roadster's upright tubes sloped back at 65 to 68 degrees, sometimes less. The rider sat literally between the wheels. A lightweight may have 72-degree angles, bringing the back wheel more beneath the saddle. A highly specialized track bike could have 77-degree angles, quite unrecognizable to the stars of the 1920s. The trend for road bikes is a degree with every decade: 72 degrees in the Sixties, 73 in the Seventies and now 74, which can prove fashionable but impractical for tall riders.

The gains are lightness (there's less tubing), responsiveness, less flexibility (with its misuse of energy) and tighter cornering. The penalties are a bumpier ride, longer handlebar extensions (increasing the strain on the head bearing and shifting the steering forward of the frame) and greater building cost. It's harder to design and build a 'steep' frame, particularly a small one. It's impossible in the smallest sizes – there's too little space for the wheels.

The tubing also differs. The cheapest bikes – those suspect bargains – have seamed tubing. Metal is rolled into tubes and welded. The system is weak for a machine which will climb hills and take corners. Sports machines have proper drawn tubing, but lightweight and racing bikes are made of butted tubing and are much lighter. Butted tubes have a similar external diameter but are hollowed in the middle where the stresses are less. The metal is chunky where it forms joints at the lugs but often as thin as eggshell in the centre. Butted tubing is more expensive; it can't be made in convenient lengths and then cut to size. It has to be drawn to set lengths and sold in boxed sets. It is also more difficult to work with, so that with the greater geometrical problems of a light frame as well, the cost of building can soar. A quality lightweight or racing frame can cost as much as a fully-equipped sports bike, but those who appreciate the difference are prepared to pay.

The biggest manufacturer of butted tubing is the British company Reynolds, whose '531' trademark turns up all over the world. Not all 531 is butted, but the transfers detail which parts of the frame are built with what.

The numbers, five, three and one are in fact the proportions of elements that go into making manganese-molybdenum steel. They first appeared in 1935 and have only recently started being challenged by other makers, notably Columbus, and by the latest product of Reynolds itself – 753 tubing of alloy steel which produces frames of exceptional lightness. There have also been experiments with all-alloy frames, even carbon fibre, but the problems are still considerable and they haven't caught on with either makers or buyers. They can also break, as happened on Eurovision during a time trial in the 1987 Tour de France.

Big factories like Raleigh make lightweight frames – Raleigh had its own professional team for many years – but most come from small makers with mundane names unknown to the wider public: Mike Mullett, Bob Jackson,

E. G. Bates, F. W. Evans . . . In many cases the builders follow the tradition of entrepreneur craftsmen working in sheds beneath railway arches – except that the shed may now occasionally be a man-and-a-boy business on a small industrial estate.

Recommendation: Buy a frame of 531 butted tubing if you can afford it. Make sure it's the right size and that there are mudguard eyes and, if you're using derailleur gears, a brazed-on gear hanger (an extension to the right side of the rear fork, on which the gear screws). The right size and good tubing is much, much more important than the colour scheme.

GEARS

Derailleur gears

Derailleur gears are a mechanical monstrosity which nobody has been able to improve. They work by twisting the chain so that it'll run on up to seven sprockets at the back and three at the front. So, in theory, you can have twenty-one gears. In fact there are rather fewer because the chain won't twist uncomplainingly to run over the extremes, and also because it's hard to stop the gears overlapping (in other words, the size of the gear may well be near-duplicated by different combinations of chainring and sprocket).

The first derailleur gears were delicate, easily broken and difficult to use. Over the years, though, they've become standard fittings, even for sports bikes, and click-stop gear levers have done away with the need to 'feel' gears into place.

Without click-stop levers (sold under different trade names), it's only a little more difficult, but you have to over-change when moving into a lower gear and under-change when going to a higher one. In other words, the subjective effect is of having to pull the lever further in one direction than in the other.

The advantages of derailleur gears is that they're cheap (at least the most inexpensive ones are; you can also buy some extremely expensive ones) and that the range of gears is almost infinitely variable. The disadvantage is that they get dirty quickly, need pretty accurate adjustment (by turning two small screws that control their inward and outward throw) and that you have to learn how to use them. Until you get the hang of them, you're prone to whizz the chain up and down the freewheel block until you find the right sprocket; hence the arrival of click-stop or indexed gear-changing. You also can't change gear while the bike is stopped, so you have to anticipate traffic lights and tight corners.

When the chain wears out, which it will after about 5,000 miles, you might also have to replace the freewheel sprockets as well. The two bed together and a new chain might jump on worn sprockets.

There are now quite a few derailleur gear-makers. The best are the Italian Campagnolo factory and the Japanese Shimano. Of particularly good value are another Japanese make, Suntour. There are no British makers.

If the chain flies off the sprockets, these are the screws to adjust. They'll look different on different makes of derailleur, but the principle's the same. The lower screw (to the right on this picture) checks the bottom gear (biggest sprocket) and the upper one the highest gear.

When you buy, check with the dealer whether the make you want has a good 'range'. Some models are made just for racing, so they can only cope with a narrow range of gears. They're small and they're light. You, on the other hand, might prefer a wider range of gears. Certainly you will if you expect to carry any amount of luggage. Firms like Campagnolo make gears with extended take-up arms, so that the gearing range can run from one-to-one right up to something suitable only for thundering down the Alps.

The standard Campagnolo racing gear has a range of 32 teeth. If you have front chainrings of 50 and 42 (a range of 8) and rear sprockets of 14–16–18–20–23–26 (a range of 12), the overall range is 8 + 12, which is well within the 32 of the Campagnolo Nuovo Record, even the 28 of the Huret Allvit.

If, though, you wanted gears which would get you both up and down the Alps, you might settle for 52 and 32 in front and 14–16–18–21–24–27 at the back. That's a range of 33, so you'd need the Simplex Prestige, with its range of 37, or the Campagnolo Gran Turismo with its unbeatable 43.

Many bikes are supplied with too high a range of gears for everyday use. Your dealer can change them for you. Look for a range from about 40 to 90 inches for ordinary riding (the system is explained on pages 140 and 141). Anything higher and lower is a bonus, unless it spaces out the gears too far.

Gear levers are usually fixed to the down tube, about eight inches back from the head tube. They're there because it makes for a convenient cable run and because, in reaching down to change gear, you're lowering the centre of gravity at a difficult moment. Alternatively, you can fix them to the handlebars, where they don't work quite as efficiently, or to the ends of dropped handlebars, which is now rare except in cyclo-cross racing.

Recommendation: Do all you can to use derailleur gears unless all you want is a bike for a few miles a day. Be sure that the range of gears goes low enough; there's no point in having a bottom gear too high for the steepest hill you'll commonly ride. Obviously that depends on whether you live in the Peaks or the Fens; your dealer will help.

Hub gears

The alternative – the only system until the 1930s – works through a collection of cogs, pawls and springs enclosed in an enlarged rear hub. The chain runs in a straight line from the chainring to the one rear sprocket, which means less wear and less friction. But hub gears provide only limited gears – usually three but occasionally one or two more – which are a set variation on each other. The commonest, the Sturmey-Archer three-speed, has a top ratio 1.33 times greater than the middle, and a bottom gear 0.75 times smaller. The middle, or second, gear is a neutral since it's the direct drive between chainring and sprocket. The German Sachs, which is making inroads, has a top 1.36 higher and a bottom of 0.73. You might also find a three-speed by the Japanese firm of Shimano.

You can alter the chainring, you can alter the sprocket, but you can't alter the relationship of gears to each other. Added to this, the normal range of a three-speed gear is generally too wide. The smallest gear tackles most hills, the highest is great for bowling along with the wind or down a prolonged drop. But for everything else, there is just one gear. On the other hand, the first man to break four hours for a 100-mile time trial, Ray Booty, chose a hub gear rather than a derailleur.

Sturmey-Archer are introducing a hub gear with more choices, but they haven't been generally available for years. The commonest, the FW, gave variations of 1.27, 1.00, 0.79 and 0.67. Others gave a narrower range.

		Ratio 1	2	3	4	5
	AW	0.75	1	1.33		
Sturmey-Archer	FM	0.67	0.89	1	1.13	
	FW	0.67	0.79	1	1.27	
	S5	0.67	0.79	1	1.27	1.50
Shimano		0.75	1	1.33		
Sachs	2	1	1.36			
	3	0.73	1	1.36		

HUB GEAR RATIOS

The other disadvantage is that hub gears are part of the wheel. Change the wheel and the replacement also has to have a hub gear. They're heavier too.

If you are wondering why anyone buys one, here's the answer: reliability. You'd have a job filling a small room with people who've had a Sturmey-Archer go wrong. And it's just as well they're made as well as they are: open one and you'll find complexity enough to make mechanics wince. They can also be moved from one gear to the other while the bike's stopped.

Sturmey-Archer's address is Lenton Boulevard, Nottingham.

Recommendation: Choose hub gears if you plan just a few miles a day, or if you'll be leaving your bike outdoors a lot, or if you're a real mechanical incompetent.

Gear ratios

However far gears have progressed, English-speakers still talk of them as though they were riding penny-farthings. On the Continent they talk of what distance the bike will travel with one turn of the pedals. We talk of the size of wheel that would turn once to travel as far – in other words, a penny-farthing wheel. This means that in the old days nobody rode gears higher than about 58 inches because nobody had an inside leg of much more than 32 inches, the distance from the saddle to the pedals at their lowest position. That's a pretty low gear for everyday riding, but of course the roads were bad. Steep descents were a danger because the pedals ran away with themselves. For many years the CTC put up 'steep hill' signs, not at the bottom but at the summit.

Speeds soared when gears arrived because leg-length was no longer the limit. Top riders now use gears of more than 100 inches. Nobody thinks of the penny-farthing when they talk of gears in inches, but that's their origin.

The formula – most people use a gear table rather than do the arithmetic themselves – is: Teeth on chainwheel × wheel size in inches ÷ teeth on rear sprocket. So, for example, $52 \times 27 \div 18 = 78$

Note: In the following tables those gears which are impractical because they are either too high or too low are printed in italics.

GEAR TABLE FOR 26-INCH WHEELS

	24	26	28	30	32	34	36	38	40	42	44	45	46	47	48	49	50	51	52	53	54
12	52	56.3	60.6	65	69.3	73.6	78	82.3	86.6	91	95.3	97.5	99.6	*101*	*104*	*106*	*108*	*111*	*113*	*115*	*117*
13	47.9	52	55.9	59.9	63.9	67.9	71.9	75.9	79.9	84	87.9	90	91.8	93.9	95.9	97.8	99.8	*102*	*104*	*106*	*108*
14	44.5	48.2	52	55.7	59.4	63.1	66.8	70.5	74.2	78	81.7	83.5	85.4	87.2	89.1	91	92.8	94.7	96.5	98.4	*100*
15	41.6	45	48.5	52	55.4	58.9	62.4	65.8	69.3	72.8	76.2	78	79.7	81.4	83.2	84.9	86.6	88.4	90.1	91.8	93.6
16	39	42.2	45.5	48.7	52	55.2	58.5	61.7	65	68.2	71.5	73.1	74.7	76.3	78	79.6	81.2	82.8	84.5	86.1	87.7
17	36.7	39.7	42.8	45.8	48.9	52	55	58.1	61.1	64.2	67.2	68.8	70.3	71.8	73.4	74.9	76.4	78	79.5	81	82.5
18	34.6	37.5	40.4	43.3	46.2	49.1	52	54.8	57.7	60.6	63.5	65	66.4	67.8	69.3	70.7	72.2	73.6	75.1	76.5	78
19	32.8	35.5	38.3	41	43.7	46.5	49.2	52	54.7	57.4	60.2	61.5	62.9	64.3	65.6	67	68.4	69.7	71.1	72.5	73.8
20	31.2	33.8	36.4	39	41.6	44.2	46.8	49.4	52	54.6	57.2	58.5	59.8	61.1	62.4	63.7	65	66.3	67.6	68.9	70.2
21	29.7	32.1	34.6	37.1	39.6	42	44.5	47	49.5	52	54.4	55.7	56.9	58.1	59.4	60.6	61.9	63.1	64.3	65.5	66.8
22	28.3	30.7	33	35.4	37.8	40.1	42.5	44.9	47.2	49.6	52	53.1	54.3	55.5	56.7	57.9	59	60.2	61.4	62.6	63.8
23	*27.1*	*29.3*	31.6	33.9	36.1	38.4	40.6	42.9	45.2	47.4	49.7	50.8	52	53.1	54.2	55.3	56.5	57.6	58.7	59.9	61
24	*26*	*28.1*	30.3	32.5	34.6	36.8	39	41.1	43.3	45.5	47.6	48.7	49.8	50.9	52	53	54.1	55.2	56.3	57.4	58.5
25	*24.9*	*27*	*29.1*	31.2	33.2	35.3	37.4	39.5	41.6	43.6	45.7	46.8	47.8	48.8	49.9	50.9	52	53	54	55.1	56.1
26	*24*	*26*	*28*	*30*	32	34	36	38	40	42	44	45	46	47	48	49	50	51	52	53	54
27	*23.1*	*25*	*26.9*	*28.8*	30.8	32.7	34.6	36.5	38.5	40.4	42.3	43.3	44.2	45.2	46.2	47.1	48.1	49.1	50	51	52
28	*22.2*	*24.1*	*26*	*27.8*	*29.7*	31.5	33.4	35.2	37.1	39	40.8	41.7	42.7	43.6	44.5	45.5	46.4	47.3	48.2	49.2	50.1
29	*21.5*	*23.3*	*25.1*	*26.8*	*28.6*	30.4	32.2	34	35.8	37.6	39.4	40.3	41.2	42.1	43	43.9	44.8	45.7	46.6	47.5	48.4
30	*20.8*	*22.5*	*24.2*	*26*	*27.7*	29.4	31.2	32.9	34.6	36.4	38.1	39	39.8	40.7	41.6	42.4	43.3	44.2	45	45.9	46.8
31	*20.1*	*21.8*	*23.4*	*25.1*	*26.8*	28.5	30.1	31.8	33.5	35.2	36.9	37.7	38.5	39.5	39.4	41	41.9	42.7	43.6	44.4	45.2
32	*19.5*	*21.1*	*22.4*	*24.3*	*26*	*27.6*	29.2	30.8	32.5	34.1	35.7	36.5	37.3	38.1	39	39.8	40.6	41.4	42.2	43	43.8

GEAR TABLE FOR 27-INCH WHEELS

	24	26	28	30	32	34	36	38	40	42	44	45	46	47	48	49	50	51	52	53	54
12	54	58.4	62.9	67.5	71.9	76.4	81	85.4	89.9	94.5	98.9	101	103	106	108	110	112	115	117	119	122
13	49.8	54	58.1	62.3	66.4	70.6	74.7	78.9	83.0	87.2	91.3	93.4	95.5	97.6	99.6	101	104	106	108	110	112
14	46.2	50.1	54	57.8	61.7	65.5	69.4	73.2	77.1	81	84.8	86.7	88.7	90.6	92.5	94.5	96.4	98.3	100	102	104
15	43.2	46.7	50.3	54	57.5	61.1	64.8	68.3	71.9	75.6	79.1	81	82.7	84.5	86.4	88.1	89.9	91.8	93.5	95.3	97.2
16	40.5	43.8	47.2	50.6	54	57.3	60.7	64.1	67.5	70.8	74.2	75.9	77.6	79.3	81	82.6	84.3	86	87.7	89.4	91.1
17	38.1	41.2	44.4	47.6	50.8	54	57.1	60.3	63.5	66.7	69.8	71.4	73.0	74.6	76.2	77.8	79.4	81	82.5	84.1	85.7
18	35.9	38.9	41.9	44.9	47.9	51	54	56.9	59.9	62.9	65.9	67.5	68.9	70.4	71.9	73.4	74.9	76.4	77.9	79.4	81
19	34.1	36.9	39.7	42.6	45.4	48.3	51.1	54	56.8	59.6	62.5	63.9	65.3	66.7	68.2	69.6	71	72.4	73.8	75.3	76.7
20	32.4	35.1	37.8	40.5	43.2	45.9	48.6	51.3	54	56.7	59.4	60.7	62.1	63.4	64.8	66.1	67.5	68.8	70.2	71.5	72.9
21	30.8	33.4	35.9	38.5	41.1	43.7	46.2	48.8	51.4	54	56.5	57.8	59.1	60.4	61.7	62.9	64.2	65.5	66.8	68.1	69.4
22	29.4	31.9	34.3	36.8	39.2	41.7	44.1	46.6	49	51.5	54	55.2	56.4	57.6	58.9	60.1	61.3	62.5	63.8	65	66.2
23	28.1	30.5	32.8	35.2	37.5	39.9	42.2	44.6	46.9	49.1	51.6	52.8	54	55.1	56.3	57.5	58.6	59.8	61	62.2	63.3
24	27	29.2	31.4	33.7	35.9	38.2	40.5	42.7	44.9	47.2	49.4	50.6	51.7	52.8	54	55.1	56.2	57.3	58.4	59.6	60.7
25	25.9	28.0	30.2	32.4	34.5	36.7	38.8	41	43.2	45.3	47.5	48.6	49.6	50.7	51.8	52.9	54	55.0	56.2	57.2	58.3
26	24.9	27	29	31.1	33.2	35.3	37.3	39.4	41.5	43.6	45.6	46.7	47.7	48.8	49.8	50.8	51.9	52.9	54	55	56
27	24	26	28	30	32	34	36	38	40	42	44	45	46	47	48	49	50	51	52	53	54
28	23.1	25	27	28.9	30.8	32.7	34.7	36.6	38.5	40.5	42.4	43.3	44.3	45.3	46.2	47.2	48.2	49.1	50.1	51.1	52
29	22.3	24.2	26	27.9	29.7	31.6	33.5	35.3	37.2	39.1	40.9	41.8	42.8	43.7	44.6	45.6	46.5	47.4	48.4	49.3	50.2
30	21.6	23.3	25.1	27	28.7	30.5	32.4	34.1	35.9	37.8	39.5	40.5	41.3	42.2	43.2	44	44.9	45.9	46.7	47.6	48.6
31	20.9	22.6	24.3	26.1	27.8	29.6	31.3	33	34.8	36.5	38.3	39.1	40	40.9	41.8	42.6	43.5	44.4	45.2	46.1	47
32	20.2	21.9	23.6	25.3	27	28.6	30.2	32	33.7	35.4	37.1	37.9	38.8	39.6	40.5	41.3	42.1	43	43.8	44.7	45.5

The Continental system refers to gear development, or more simply, how far a gear will roll with one turn of the pedals. The formula is: Metric wheel circumference × teeth on chainring ÷ teeth on sprocket.

GEAR TABLE, CONTINENTAL-STYLE, FOR 700MM WHEELS

	40	41	42	43	44	45	46	47	48	49	50	51	52	53	54
13	6.57	6.73	6.90	7.06	7.23	7.39	7.55	7.72	7.88	8.05	8.21	8.38	8.54	8.70	8.87
14	6.10	6.25	6.40	6.56	6.71	6.86	7.01	7.17	7.32	7.47	7.63	7.78	7.93	8.08	8.23
15	5.69	5.84	5.98	6.12	6.26	6.40	6.55	6.69	6.83	6.97	7.12	7.26	7.40	7.54	7.68
16	5.34	5.47	5.60	5.74	5.87	6.00	6.14	6.27	6.40	6.54	6.67	6.81	6.94	7.07	7.20
17	5.02	5.15	5.27	5.40	5.52	5.65	5.78	5.90	6.03	6.15	6.28	6.40	6.53	6.66	6.78
18	4.74	4.86	4.98	5.10	5.22	5.34	5.45	5.57	5.69	5.81	5.93	6.05	6.17	6.29	6.41
19	4.50	4.61	4.72	4.83	4.94	5.05	5.17	5.28	5.39	5.50	5.62	5.73	5.84	5.95	6.07
20	4.27	4.37	4.48	4.59	4.70	4.80	4.91	5.02	5.12	5.23	5.34	5.44	5.55	5.66	5.76
21	4.07	4.17	4.27	4.37	4.47	4.57	4.67	4.78	4.88	4.98	5.08	5.18	5.29	5.39	5.49
22	3.88	3.98	4.07	4.17	4.27	4.37	4.46	4.56	4.66	4.75	4.85	4.95	5.04	5.14	5.24
23	3.71	3.80	3.90	3.99	4.08	4.18	4.27	4.36	4.45	4.55	4.64	4.73	4.83	4.92	5.01
24	3.56	3.64	3.73	3.82	3.91	4.00	4.09	4.18	4.27	4.36	4.45	4.54	4.62	4.71	4.80
25	3.42	3.50	3.58	3.67	3.76	3.84	3.93	4.01	4.10	4.18	4.27	4.35	4.44	4.52	4.61
26	3.28	3.36	3.45	3.53	3.61	3.69	3.78	3.86	3.94	4.02	4.10	4.19	4.27	4.35	4.43

12. I've Been This Way Before

There is no such thing as a 'best' bike. Those consumer magazines that tell you there is ought to know better. There may be factories somewhere that turn out absolutely consistent machines, with identical accessories, but I bet there aren't many of them. Most bikes are made in the way that cars are: with continual small changes. So, although your Featherweight Super-Racer bought in Southampton will be *similar* to the one you saw the previous week in Ayr, there's no reason to suppose it's identical.

Since components come with their worth pretty closely attached to their price, you can also fairly assume that bikes of the same price from different manufacturers will be of similar quality. So, if the shop doesn't have the make you wanted, it's better to look at what's available there before you make the long journey somewhere else.

SECONDHAND BIKES

But what happens when you buy secondhand?

The old rule to be wary obviously applies. While few bike shops would swindle you, nor are they going to have the same respect for an old bike as for a new one. Those shops that do actually sell secondhand bikes only took them unwillingly in the first place as a part exchange – unwillingly because the profit on new bikes is a much lower percentage than any other retailer would consider. So whether you buy from a shop or privately, these are the things to check:

The frame – Stand back and look at it. Never buy a frame that's in the slightest way bent. Bent forks can be replaced, but the impact might well have weakened the tubing, even though it hasn't bent it. Run your finger under the top and down tubes about three inches back from the head tube. That's where a frame bends. Feel for tell-tale cracks in the paintwork. If that's fine, try to judge whether the frame is in track – in other words, if the wheels follow each other. One good test is to try to ride it hands-off. It's extremely difficult to do it on an out-of-track frame. Don't buy an obviously neglected frame – one with extensive paint damage (as distinct from acceptable wear and tear). Flaked and badly scraped paint show lack of care and attention from previous owners.

The wheels – Spin them and see how true they are. Small deflections can be corrected if the spokes aren't rusted, but anything more than quarter of an inch suggests ill-use. Don't buy a bike with rusted spokes, or with spokes missing (look round the rim for spoke-less holes – it's a bad sign). Now try sideways movement in the hub. Hold the rim steady and wobble the rim sideways. Be very dubious about more than the slightest play. The problem might just be poor adjustment, but it could also indicate wear. Don't buy steel rims, if only for the simple reason that alloy ones are better and really don't cost much more. Rebuilding a pair of wheels with new, stainless spokes would cost about £30; rebuilding with new rims, perhaps £45.

The tyres – Tyres can be replaced and would have to be eventually, anyway. But badly worn tyres, especially tyres with the canvas showing, mean neglect which could indicate problems elsewhere.

The transmission – Do the gears work? Lift the back wheel, get someone else to turn the pedals, and *you* operate the gears. They should engage securely and smoothly in every ratio. There should be not the slightest trace of rust on the chain. It shouldn't lift more than fractionally at its tightest point from the chainring. Chains wear anyway and a replacement would cost about £6 – but remember that you might also have to replace the derailleur sprockets. Is there play in the bottom bracket? Wobble the cranks sideways to find out. Again, slight play might mean poor adjustment. Anything more than a hint, and certainly any clicking noises as the cranks turn, could mean wear. Bottom bracket damage increases in cost with the quality of the chainset you've got to renovate. Now look sideways at the chainring and the rear sprockets. Slight wear in the outline of the teeth is acceptable, but any hooking or concave shape is unacceptable, especially if the chainring doesn't detach from the crank.

The brakes – Do they work? Are they smooth? It pays to replace brake blocks and cables, anyway – the expense is minor – so all you're interested in is how well they work.

The steering – Apply the front brake and push the bike forward. The head bearing is poorly adjusted if the bike rocks. Insist on having it correctly adjusted, because poor adjustment might be disguising a pitted ball race. Now lift the front wheel by supporting the bike by the frame, and turn the handlebars gently as far as they'll go in both directions. The headset will need replacing (£8–25) if there's any feeling of the steering clicking across – a sign that the headset is pitted and the ball-bearings are running from one little hole to the next. Just replacing the ball-bearings or slackening the headset won't cure the problem (indeed, it'll make it worse).

There are enough good bikes around for you not to have to trouble with anything that fails the test. The cost of replaced wheels, tyres, headset, chain and sprockets could easily mean the difference between the price of your secondhand 'bargain' and a new bike. The profit on a new bike is only in the region of a third – from which the dealer has to run, light, heat and insure his shop, pay his rates and his staff, and make enough money to order new stock at increased prices – so there's little room to haggle over prices. On the other hand, it does mean that when a dealer offers you an unsolicited reduction in price, he's doing you a genuine favour. He certainly hasn't marked the price up in the first place, as the used car world does, to make the reduction possible.

Secondhand bikes come cheapest from the lad in the next street who's got all he wants from his old machine and wants to clear it out. They're the bikes you see advertised in shop windows and local papers. The value of old bikes nosedives when they're not looked after, whereas a cared-for bike will hold half its list price for years. Don't be fooled into buying a cheap dud.

RESPRAYS

Finally, if you want your secondhand bargain resprayed, remember that it's a specialist job – you *can* do it yourself but only with much trouble and an inferior finish – and that you'll normally be expected to strip all the components off the bike. A dealer will do this for you, but naturally he'll expect to be paid for his time. He'll also expect to send the frame off to the enameller for you, not least because he then gets a percentage commission.

It doesn't usually work out any cheaper to take your frame directly to the sprayer, but it might work out a little quicker. The main bike specialists include:

Ellis-Briggs, of 18 Otley Road, Shipley, West Yorkshire BD17 7DS (0274–583221).

Bob Jackson, 148 Harehills Lane, Leeds LS8 5BD (0532–493022).

Mercian Cycles, 7 Shardlow Road, Alvaston, Derby DE2 0JG (0332–752468).

Miracle Finishes, 60 Radium Street, Ancoates, Manchester 4 (061–236 9254 or 061–228 0639).

M. Steel Lightweights, Old Northumberland Yard, Wallsend, Tyne and Wear (091–234 4275).

Vaz Finishes, London SE13 6SP (01–852 0711).

13. In This Land of Darkness

Late one Friday night, I set off, despite dreadful warnings, to ride through the darkness to the south coast. We'd often gone on family holidays to a caravan site near Eastbourne and I had fond memories of the area. I was warned about being cold. I was warned about endless drunks who'd be cruising the road hungrily for me after closing time. I was warned about having enough to eat, too little to drink . . .

London was quiet as I slipped through in the small hours, out past the fledgling airport at Gatwick, where red-eyed girls puffed up their hairdos and kicked off their shoes, and then on through the lanes to join the main Eastbourne road. They were right about it being cold. Once, I stopped in a telephone kiosk with a hurricane lamp for warmth, cursing my idea of wearing shorts on a summer's night. Later I was stopped at a road block by policemen looking for an escaped convict. They shared their coffee with me and all was well. I stayed in a room full of dead butterflies at Alfriston youth hostel and pedalled back through Lewes and Pease Pottage next day.

Since then I've ridden through the darkness many times, always more comfortably, always better dressed. It's pleasant on summer evenings when it's warm and light till late, but in the winter it's often dark by 4pm.

BATTERY LIGHTS

In all the time I've been riding a bike, I've never been able to decide which lighting I prefer. There's something odd about the bicycle industry in that it leaves outsiders to make battery lamps. You can buy the most beautifully crafted chainsets and precision gears and then have to settle for battery lamps which fall to pieces or, at best, need cardboard stuffed in them to dim the rattle. Truthfully, I can say that, with the exception of French Wonderlights, I've never had a set of battery lights that didn't rattle and with which I felt happy riding without elastic bands to keep them from exploding.

Wonderlights – slim, flat boxes – have my confidence. They do, though, use slim, flat batteries which aren't so easy to buy as the ubiquitous U2 cells, and which cost rather more. Never under-estimate the cost of running battery lights. And if you *do* use U2-type cells, buy the more expensive Duracell black version. You'll spend more in the first place but they'll outlast the normal blue cells by far. Ordinary batteries will give you just two or three hours of continuous use, or less in cold weather (which is when you'll want them most). Nothing is more infuriating, or dangerous, than to have a rear light that grows dim or, worse, flickers on and off. My vote goes to Wonderlights. The fastenings are ugly, the batteries are inconvenient, but they *work*!

There is, very slowly, a move towards cyclists answering their own problems. A few have set up on their own and started making rechargeable batteries. Billington make a set called Nightfarer, for example, and M.V.B. make their Owl system (M.V.B. Components, Unit 9, Station Road, Ware SG12 7BS; 0920-2736). They're still batteries, of course, so they do run out – most rechargeable batteries don't go through a dimming stage before they give up, which is worrying – but the eventual cost is lower.

By the way, remove any removable battery lights when you stop in cities before somebody else does. It's a pain, walking about the place with all the loose bits – pump, lights etc. – but the consolation is that if you're wearing funny specialist clothes, it does give the rest of the world an explanation.

Ken Matthews, who's an enthusiast in the west country, came up with a novel solution to wondering whether your back light is still on. It's only worthwhile if you use battery lights all year. He bought a length of fibre optic cable, which is now much cheaper than it was, and slipped one end into the lens casing of the back light. The rest of the cable he then led back up the bike, along the brake cable or in some other convenient place, until it reached the handlebars. He could then see the tiny fibre end glowing all the time the back light stayed alight. Clever, eh? The alternative is to look round every couple of miles, or to watch your reflection in shop windows.

DYNAMOS

I have a love–hate relationship with dynamos. I'm in the love stage at the moment. Dynamos come in three types – bottle dynamos, which run on the side walls of the tyre; barrel dynamos which run on the tread; and hub dynamos, which are enclosed, as you might imagine, in the hub. They all produce much more light than battery lamps, but they all have disadvantages:

Bottle dynamos create a fair bit of drag. The newer and very old ones are best, and probably the drag is much worse subjectively as you get more tired. The friction wheel wears faster than the tyre, surprisingly, (except on the very lightest tyres, which have no protected sidewall), so it's worth fitting a rubber or plastic cover. The cover slightly reduces the output by enlarging and therefore slowing the little wheel, and it changes the sound from a whirr to a faint whine.

Barrel dynamos are often criticized for slipping in the rain and, especially, in the snow. They are normally fitted to the chainstays, immediately behind the bottom bracket, where they're neater than the rather ugly bottle dynamos but more prone to road muck. They run on the tyre rim, so there's less wear than with a bottle model, because they're running in line rather than always slightly scuffing the tyre wall. On the other hand, the lack of scuffing produces a weaker contact that's much more dependent on the tyre being absolutely concentric and not building up too much surface water.

Hub dynamos have no friction at all and make no noise. They're unaffected by water or any other sort of weather. And, if you can put up with the weight and clutter, it is possible to connect them to standby batteries for when you stop. The disadvantages are: the supply is erratic and getting worse because they're no longer made in quantity; they're heavy; and they need to be built into a special wheel which might not fit lightweight frames easily. They also can't be removed without changing the wheel.

My own experience is solely with barrel dynamos. The front light is so much stronger than a battery lamp that motorists dip their headlights. The light is even stronger now that halogen lamps are available. But dynamos are made mainly for everyday cyclists. Ride them at all enthusiastically and you blow the bulbs. You then have to fit higher value bulbs which, of course, dim more quickly as you slow down.

With my original dynamo I used to have a puzzling fault which finally led me to abandon it. I had uprated the bulbs and they never blew as I rode. But if I stopped at a shop, one bulb had always blown when it came to start off again. Even uprating hadn't stopped the filament overheating and then cracking as it cooled. This puzzled me because it hadn't happened when I first got the dynamo. Then I realized it was probably no more than my fitness increasing and my overall riding speed going up a mile or two an hour. That was all that was needed.

I abandoned the dynamo and I went back to batteries, swearing at their cost and unreliability, until my wife gave me a new one for Christmas. As someone versed in electronics and aware of my earlier problems, she'd had the initiative to buy a little gadget, about the size of wrapped sugar lumps, which stopped power surges getting through to the bulbs. Oh joy! No blown bulbs, loads of blazing light, utter reliability. Still the odd slip in the rain if I don't get the tension and the positioning just right (down the sidewall a bit, rather than up near the tread, where the water sweeps), but what an improvement . . .

Even so, I still carry spare bulbs, wrapped in tissue and pushed into the handlebar ends. You'll need 6V 0.45 or 0.5A front bulbs and 6V 0.1A rear bulbs for tyre-driven dynamos, the same front bulbs for Dynohubs but 6V 0.25A for the front. Make sure the fittings match your dynamo. If the bulbs fail or they get black quickly, fit new ones, 0.05A higher.

If the lights flicker, check the wiring. Most tyre-driven dynamos have one 'live' wire and use the frame for the earth, connecting through a sharp-ended screw which pierces the paintwork to touch bare metal. It works fine in theory but can be erratic in practice. A lot of riders prefer to have a second, return wire. Earthing problems are the main cause for flickering lights.

REFLECTORS

There are other gadgets for the night-time cyclist. The reflective Sam Brown belt is one. There are spoke reflectors as well, which went from being illegal to being compulsory on new bikes, almost overnight. Your dealer has to fit them if you buy a complete machine from him, but you can remove them immediately if you wish. You can, he can't. Crazy. In time they'll probably be obligatory, anyway.

I also fit pedal reflectors to my winter bike. They're essential in Belgium, which is where I first used them, and I value them highly. Cycle lights are more to be seen than to see by, and moving lights attract more attention than immobile ones. Reflectors create a distinctive pattern in car lights. So, too, do Matex arm or leg lamps which a lot of Continentals use. They're illegal here, because lights have to be fixed to the machine and not the rider, and I've only seen them on sale infrequently. They look a little like the gadgets doctors use for peering into ears – a slender barrel to house batteries and a small lamp unit on top with a white lens on one side and a red one on the other. If you are cycling abroad strap one to your arm or, better still, the top of your calf and you will weave a wondrous pattern as you go.

DAZZLE

Apart from making yourself seen, the problem of riding at night is the contrast between headlamps and darkness. It won't bother you in street lighting – or at least only occasionally – but it can be a real problem cycling on unlit roads. Most motorists who spot your headlight, particularly a dynamo light, will dip their lights. But some won't. Some might not even see you on the other side of the road.

If you get dazzled, keep looking down. You can gauge the offside by the position of the oncoming lights; unless you look down, you won't see the verge. If you *do* lose the edge of the road, do one of two things. Either stop (which oddly enough is risky, because it takes some distance to come to a standstill, in which time you might hit something) or ride out towards but not in the path of the lights. The nearer you get to the lights, the further you'll be from the verge or kerb. If something comes up from behind, the approaching lights should make your villain dip his lights. If this doesn't work, you might be able to achieve the same with a lot of dramatic waving and fist shaking.

Finally, as any car comes alongside from the opposite direction, close your eyes for a second to readjust to the change in light.

14. When Things Go Wrong

Oh yes, bikes will work without attention. They're not like cars. You can ride about for year after year, for decades on end, and about the only things that will actually wear to destruction are the tyres. Everything else will get rustier and more worn and stiffer, but will at least *work*. The only penalty is that the engine – you – have to work harder and harder. And one day, the bike will catch you out.

TYRES

Punctures

The old engineers didn't always get it right. The magazine *The Engineer* in February 1890 credited pneumatic tyres as being 'the most conspicuous innovation in cycle construction,' but they had doubts: 'Considerable difficulty will be experienced in keeping the tyres thoroughly inflated [and] they are prone to slip on muddy roads . . . The appearance of the tyres destroys the symmetry and graceful appearance of a cycle, and this alone is, we think, sufficient to prevent their coming into general use.'

Conventional tyres are called wired-ons because the edges contain a strand of wire to keep their shape and size. In fact, the wire these days is sometimes non-metallic, making it easier to fold. You have to remove the outer cover with tyre levers. Nothing you can bodge will be as good, although teaspoons with broad-ended handles are the next best thing.

Start at the site of the puncture. You might have to pump up the tyre a bit to hear the air escaping. Let the rest of the air out by opening the valve and pinch the tyre together at the site of the hole. Slide the straight end of the tyre lever down the side of the rim and under the edge of the tyre and lever it back, using the wall of the rim as a fulcrum.

The tyre probably won't come all the way and you'll need a second lever to get it over the rim wall. Many levers have a slot at the angled end to hook over a spoke, letting you concentrate on each lever in turn without running out of hands. Lifting the tyre is difficult at first – it has to be a tight fit or the cover would blow off – but it gets easier as you free a few inches.

Remove about eight inches of tyre on just one side and feel inside for the inner tube. Pull out as much as will come free. Now reinflate the tube and listen for the air. If you got it right, you can go straight to the section on mending the hole. If you guessed wrongly, you might as well remove the whole inner tube. To do this, you need to remove the whole wheel. (See the section on wheels for details.) Having taken off the wheel, undo the lock ring that tightens the valve to the rim and keep it safely. Carry on right round the wheel until all one side of the tyre is off the rim. Push the valve back up through its hole in the rim and remove the inner tube completely.

Inflate the inner tube again and it should now be obvious where the hole is. If it isn't – if the leak is especially slow – pump the tube a lot more (it'll take a very great deal to burst it) and roll and stretch it as you pass it by your ear. Your eyeball is sensitive to escaping air if you *think* you've found the hole. Mark the puncture with a ballpoint pen. If you can't do this, keep your fingertip close to the hole and deflate the tube. Holes disappear when you let the air out, so don't lose track of it.

Most inner tubes are made of artificial rubber. The patch won't stick unless you remove the bloom from the surface. But pure rubber (latex) tubes don't have this bloom, so if you have one you can ignore this next bit.

With an artificial tube, scratch a faint cross over the hole with a piece of sandpaper. Then rub the surface thoroughly in whatever shape and area you want, so long as the hole is in the middle of it and you've scraped an area larger than the patch you plan to use. Sandpaper is the best, but in an emergency I've used a rough stone and even the road surface.

Smear puncture solution evenly over the roughened patch of tube, again with the hole in the middle and over an area slightly larger than the patch. Smooth the solution with your finger and let the glue dry. This is important because the patch won't stick if you don't let the solution dry completely. It'll take a couple of minutes (although less on a hot day).

As soon as it's dry, peel a patch off its metallic backing. Many patches have a strip of transparent material on the non-gummed side – don't try to remove it yet. Press the patch on to the dry solution, again with the hole in the middle, and press it down firmly, especially at the edges. Press for a minute or so, rolling your thumb over the whole area, and then fold the patch downwards so that the remaining strip of material cracks. Peel it off from the middle outwards, taking care not to lift the edges of the patch. Get rid of as much surplus dry solution as you can by rubbing your fingertips over it or, if you've got it, sprinkling powdered chalk on it.

If you've stuck the patch on properly, you won't need to test the tube by pumping it up. I always prefer not to because it weakens the adhesion by stretching the tube. It's a nuisance to have got the tube back into the cover and the cover on the rim before finding something's wrong, but on the other hand it's even more galling to loosen a satisfactory patch.

Something caused the puncture, so run your fingers inside the cover before you replace the tube. The thorn or flint or whatever might still be sticking through the tread. Look and feel carefully and remove anything suspicious.

It's rare that a puncture will leave a large hole in the tread, but it's possible.

Repair kits used to contain a small piece of waterproofed canvas for this eventuality, but by this stage you're into first aid rather than repairs, so anything is better than nothing – even a strip of handkerchief, or a large puncture patch. Whatever you use, stuff it *inside* the tyre, between the inner tube and the cover. Anything you put outside the tyre will wear away, come loose and jam the works in no time.

Now you have to replace the inner tube. If you removed just a few inches, simply push them back into place. If you removed the whole lot, push the valve back through the hole and push as much of the inner tube as you can roughly into place. You'll soon find that it won't go very well. So, starting opposite the valve, push in a few inches and hold them in place by easing the tyre edges over the rim wall. Carry on round the wheel. Eventually you'll be in the same position as you would have been had you removed only a few inches.

The last inches are always the hardest. Pinch the cover until it drops into the well of the rim. Then put the unfitted section of tyre on the ground and stretch the tyre downwards. Use your thumbs to push the rest of the tyre over the rim. Make sure you haven't trapped any of the inner tube by mistake.

Some tyres are easier than others. Do all you can to complete the job with your thumbs. If you just can't, use the tyre levers again. But take very great care, and pump a few strokes of air into the inner tube before you use them. It's very difficult, even for an expert, to replace an outer cover without pinching the inner tube with the tyre levers and putting fresh holes into the tube.

If you removed all the tyre, you'll end up at the valve. Push it back up through the hole until only the last third shows. That'll get the base out of the way. Refit the last inches of tyre and pull the valve back down, fixing it in place with the lock nut. Then replace and reinflate the tyre.

Hints: Take a spare inner tube with you. It's easier to replace a whole inner tube and mend the punctured one at home. This is especially so in the rain because patches don't stick as well in damp weather.

Puncture solution isn't dear, so don't hesitate to apply a second thin layer once the first has dried. Let that dry, too, and the patch will stick even better.

Valves

Inner tubes are fitted with one of three basic valves. The oldest version still in use is the Woods, recognizable by a central, knurled, locking ring which screws a quarter of the way down the valve body, leaving a thinner, threaded body protruding. The knurled ring is slackened a little, the pump is connected and the air rushes up the inside of the smaller portion, out of a small hole in the side, and into the inner tube by blowing open a thin tube of rubber. The Woods valve can only take whatever air pressure can be resisted by the elasticity of the rubber tubing. Pump in any more and the air simply flows back into the pump as you draw back the handle.

In the end, anyway, the rubber perishes or just gives up the ghost, which is why small tubes of rubber were supplied for many years in puncture repair kits. The rubber is still available, but you might find it simpler to replace the inner tube with a different model and be done with it.

The valve found increasingly on medium-priced and most children's bikes is the Schraeder, which is just about the same as a car tyre valve. The air-stopping mechanism is inside the valve and is pushed outwards, stopping the air escaping, by the air pressure itself. It will therefore take potentially higher pressures, but it is susceptible to uneven fits and slow leaks.

You can pump Schraeder valves from petrol filling station pumps, but it's inadvisable for two reasons. The first is that garage air-lines have unreliable pressure gauges. The second is that most of them will pump air to a much higher pressure than the bicycle tyre was ever intended to take, and there have been tales of tyres disintegrating under too much air accidentally inserted. I have never heard this tale substantiated, but the possibility is worrying enough. This higher pressure (only the soggiest of bike tyres takes less pressure than a car) doesn't matter much to motorists because the volume of a car tyre is much greater and therefore takes longer to fill, making mishaps much less likely.

The handiest gadget that ever cut a cyclist's labours is called a track pump, which looks like an old-fashioned stirrup pump (an upright tube with a double-handled plunger in the top). It pumps air at high pressure, via a pressure gauge, into a rubber tube and through a push-on adaptor into the tyre. It costs about the same as two or three wired-on tyres, but, by golly, it cuts the effort of pumping to almost nothing.

The better production bikes and those belonging to enthusiasts are fitted with Presta valves. These are the slenderest of the three and easily recognized by the tiny locknut which screws down on top. Like the Schraeder, they work by having an internal plunger being pushed shut by the internal air pressure. The locknut is there to ensure a tight fit and minimal leakage. Presta valves cannot be used at garage pressure pumps, but they're the standard fitting for all decent bicycle pumps and for track pumps. They tend to be available in only the standard adult inner tube sizes and my advice, if you've got valves of another sort, is to change the inner tubes for Prestas. Take care, though, because the rim hole for Schraeder and Woods valves is larger and you'll have to fit a slender and smooth-edged washer inside the rim to stop the Presta valve forcing its way out.

Schraeder valves also use a differently sized adaptor.

If a valve ever goes wrong (other than the rubber perishing on a Woods valve), there's no practical alternative to buying a new valve.

Tyre pressure

The wheels take a hammering as you ride because they support you, transmit your power to the ground, resist braking strains, and stand up to sudden twisting and sideways stress. Some changes in the pressure come suddenly as a result of, say, whacking the bike into something else, or cornering too tightly, but most are gradual changes, so tyre pressure needs regular and frequent checks.

Test the pressure in the tyres before each ride, either by squeezing the sidewalls between fingers and thumb (never by pressing down on the tread) or by using a bicycle pressure gauge. There's a gauge on track pumps and most outer covers are marked with the optimum pressure. Curiously, you can buy identical covers in Britain and abroad and find they're marked with different pressures. Quite why, I don't know.

Most riders learn the feel of a fully-pumped tyre quickly and know with one squeeze whether it needs more air. But you can never be sure it's fully pumped if you don't know what the ideal pressure is in the first place. I do encourage you to spend a few pounds on a track pump. Not only will you save energy pumping, you'll also save energy riding.

Riding tyres too soft – the usual fault – makes progress harder, wears the tread more, and slowly breaks down the sidewalls. Riding them too hard makes the bike too rigid and might, in the really exceptional cases, lift the tyre right off the rim or increase damage that already exists in the sidewall.

In a perfect world, tyres and rims would be made by the same manufacturer. They're not, of course, and when you're buying tyres it's wise to ask whether they're known for being slightly under- or over-sized for the rims you use. The sizing of bicycle tyres is quite bewildering; the nominal size of 26, 27 inches or 700mm has precious little to do with the size of either the rim or the tyre. What's more, tyres can be fitted over or under-width to rims, with certain benefits and drawbacks.

It's just the thing you wish the International Standards Organization would sort out. In fact, the ETRTO (European Tyre and Rim Technical Organization) *is* trying, but the results haven't filtered through to bike shops yet. When they do, you'll be able to specify a rim and a tyre that fit each other exactly, and you won't have to worry that the Imperial and French systems are nominal and not accurate.

All I can say is that it usually works out okay, but it's always worth asking whether the dealer has any inside knowledge.

EQUIVALENT TYRE SIZES AND DIAMETERS

IMPERIAL	FRENCH	ETRTO	Diameters of available tyre widths*						
			20	25	28	32	37	40	44
27 × 1¼	—	630	670	680	686	694			
28 × 1⅝	700C	622	662	672	678	686	696	702	710
26 × 1¼	—	597				661			
26 × 1⅜	650A	590				654	664		
26 × 1½	650B	584				648	658	664	672
* ± 6mm									

Source: *Cycletouring*, April 1986

The greater the ideal pressure, the greater the gradual deflation and the more obvious the effects on riding. Low-pressure tyres, like those on children's bikes and some shopping models, leak as well but more slowly. Check before each ride and top up the air, weekly with butyl tubes, daily with pure rubber ones.

A recent trend has been to add reinforcement to tyres to make punctures less likely. The usual way is to add an extremely thin strip of a substance called Kevlar immediately under the centre of the tread. At first this made the tyres a little 'peaky' – in other words, nearing on the triangular, and not so easy to take corners. Now the problem's been solved and, although reports of the degree of puncture resistance vary, they ride much more smoothly. These tyres cost rather more, though. One of the most prominent makers are Nutrak with their Beltguard tyres.

Less recommended are the reinforced belts that you can fit yourself between the inner tube and the outer cover. Too many people have reported problems with the tapes slipping, ridging the tyres and even causing punctures with their frayed edges.

Hints: If you get a lot of punctures, fit heavier tyres. But also consider a tyre-saver, a thin piece of metal tubing that runs along the tread and whips out thorns and other nuisances before they penetrate the rubber. Most tyre-savers are made for racing bikes without mudguards, but you can get mudguard-fitting versions from Tag Products at Unit 1, 12 Carlton Way, Cambridge CB4 1XN.

WHEELS

Removing the wheels

The front wheel is simple. It's just a question of undoing the nuts or slipping open the quick-release lever (it'll be quite stiff, so give it a good tug). The wheel should then drop out with a firm tap (make sure you don't knock the brake blocks out as the wheel comes free).

The back wheel will slide out of its slots if you have a fixed gear (i.e. you can't freewheel), a hub gear or no gear at all. If you ride derailleur gears, put the bike into top gear (smallest rear sprocket) before you undo the wheel fixing. You might then have to swivel the derailleur back a little and turn the jockey wheel cage (the assembly holding the two small guide wheels) to clear the chain from the block; alternatively, the back wheel may come out just as simply as the front – it's all a matter of luck and good engineering.

Rear wheels with hub gears should slide out without difficulty, but in this case you should put the gear lever into its neutral position (the middle of three gears) and then unscrew the connection where the cable joins the toggle chain by the hub. The cable has to be reconnected at the end, so make sure you tighten it by exactly the same amount as you loosened it. Remember how many turns of the connection there were or, better, remember the position of the connection between the toggle chain and the pull-out rod, visible through the circular hole in the bolt flange.

Buckled wheels

Every so often spin a wheel gently and watch it from the top and the side. Looking from above will show the more usual form of buckling – side-to-side movement. Looking from the side will show whether the wheel is still a circle or has developed a flat in the rim and a faint D shape.

Don't let the tyre mislead you, because the tread edges aren't always laid perfectly evenly. Much better to watch the wall of the rim in relation to the brake block. A small variation in either direction probably won't be important. In fact, it may even be inevitable with cheaper wheels. But any substantial movement should be attended to straight away. The cause (apart from permanent damage to the rim) will always be uneven stress in the spokes.

Look first for broken spokes. Spin the wheel slowly and let the spokes tap against a finger nail. Each spoke should produce the same tone as its neighbour (although spokes on either side of a dished rear wheel will produce different notes). Listen carefully for dull clunks that indicate a broken spoke. Take broken spokes out straight away. To ride with one is to invite the others to start breaking as well.

In theory, you can replace a spoke and re-use the nipple. What happens in practice is that the old spoke either rusts or moulds itself into the thread. This is a nuisance if you are making repairs on the road because it wastes extra minutes while you remove part or all of the tyre. At home, you might as well shrug and accept that a new spoke deserves a new nipple anyway.

The job is simpler if the spoke has broken in the front wheel or the left side of the back one. Unless you've got a hub gear, to repair a spoke on the gear side of the back wheel usually means taking off the freewheel. This isn't a straightforward job and although it takes just a few minutes, it needs a special tool and a long wrench. The tool – a cross between a spanner and a screwdriver, but sometimes splined – is specific to the make of freewheel.

Remove the quick-release or nut, fit the block-remover to the block (usually locating two pins in slots but occasionally by sliding the splines together) and then tighten the quick-release or nut again. Leave a little play in the tightness.

Place the wrench on the face of the block-remover and turn it anti-clockwise so that the block loosens. Slacken the quick-release or nut a little more and repeat until the block is off.

The chances of having a foot-long wrench are remote, of course. Garages will often help. Otherwise, the best option is to knock on a door and ask. In the country you might find you can wedge the block-remover in a gate or a gully cover, turning the wheel and using its leverage to slacken the block. But be warned – it's not easy. It might be better to swear and curse and bend the spoke, bodge the job and then get it sorted out at a bike shop.

The spoke has to be precisely the right length for the wheel; it's a good idea to have half a dozen in reserve. Remove the broken spoke by pushing one end through the hole in the hub flange and the other up through the rim, from which the tyre, inner tube and rim tape have been removed. Take the new spoke and push it, threaded end first, through the flange hole. Remember to press it through in the same direction as the one you removed – you'll see that spokes run alternately from the inside and outside.

Thread the new spoke through the wheel in the same pattern as the next spoke but one round the hub. If that spoke goes under and over the spokes that it crosses, take the replacement the same way. You'll probably have to flex the spoke quite a lot to make it go the right way, but it doesn't matter so long as you don't actually *bend* it and provided you don't flex it right down at the 90-degree angle by the spoke-head.

Push the spoke nipple down through the hole in the rim, working from the outside, and tighten it on to the thread at the end of the spoke. Use a spoke key (never pliers) and tighten the spoke into place until tapping it produces the same sound as all the others. Then spin the wheel and watch for deviations. Tighten or slacken *only* the new spoke until the wobble disappears.

Now look down the hole through the rim and see how far your new spoke pokes through. If it was the right length, it will neither stick beyond the level of the rim, nor will you have used all the thread. If it does stick through for any reason, and by the minutest amount, file the spoke away (a fiddly job) until it will no longer press into the inner tube. Protruding spokes guarantee punctures. Now refit the rim tape and the inner tube and tyre (see the section on punctures). Note, though, that there is no separate rim tape on tubular tyres, although the rest of the procedure is exactly the same.

If you leave the repair too long, the other spokes start loosening independently as the rim starts to flex minutely at the unsupported place. The same thing happens if you bash into something and give the wheel a good shaking. The erratic tension produces a much more exotic kind of buckle and it's a good deal harder to get rid of. The technique to correct it is basically a matter of tightening and occasionally loosening spokes, sometimes several at a time. Remember that tightening a spoke on one side of the wheel has the same affect as slackening one on the other, but the aim should be to give all the spokes the same tension. Do this yourself if you feel confident, but beware the commonest error, which is to chase the buckle round the rim, slackening and tightening until the spokes are too floppy, too tight or a mixture of the two. At this stage you will want to do what it might have been better to have done in the first place, which is to concede that good wheel building is beyond most amateurs and the rightful work of a bike shop mechanic. I'd suggest you yourself didn't try to cure any wobble of more than half an inch, and you may decide that even half an inch is much too much.

Sometimes the wobble will go beyond what can be cured by adjustments to the spokes. Hitting a kerb or riding into a pot-hole or a brick wall might permanently change the shape of the rim, in one or two ways. Sometimes the damage might be just a slight flattening of the circle, which can be disguised although never removed by spoke adjustments. But sometimes the tyre will have compressed enough to squash up against the rim edges, so that they strike the road (or wall) and splay outwards.

Any large splaying of the rim walls is a terminal case. There's nothing to do but throw the whole rim away and buy another. You can at least have a go at small damage points, though. Small bulges which make your brakes snatch can sometimes be removed by squeezing the rim very gently and progressively in a smooth-faced vice or a C-clamp. If the bulge is on just one side, spread the load of the vice on the undamaged side by using a strip of strong wood. Otherwise you'll smooth one side and dent the other. Still smaller variations can sometimes be cured by easing them out with a small pair of grips or the jaws of a small spanner.

Watch carefully, though, for any signs of cracking or wrinkling, because jobs like this are extreme rescue attempts and may weaken the wheel beyond safe use. If in doubt, take any problem to a skilled mechanic.

If a wheel buckles really badly on the road (the commonest cause, apart from collision, is to turn the front wheel too sharply and ride 'over' it), you have no choice but a bodged repair. Happily, these work surprisingly often, especially with alloy rims. If the wheel's taken a shallow figure-of-eight shape, take it out of the frame, place the axle end on the road, grasp the rim where it sticks highest, and push it down sharply. It will usually snap back into something approximating its original shape. You then have to decide whether to re-tighten the spokes and take a chance (although I know at least one wheel that lasted for years after this happened) or leave well alone. In emergencies, remember, you may have to ride only as far as a railway station or a telephone box.

The CTC doesn't offer a 'get-you-home' service like the motoring clubs, but it does offer a network of enthusiasts who'll help you out of a fix. Their enthusiasm and time is free but the bits aren't, naturally. The service works on the basis that you'll return the favour some day to somebody else.

Adjusting wheel cones

The wheels rotate on a ring of ball-bearings in the hub. If a bearing is too loose, the wheel wears; if it is too tight, the wheel wears even faster. How tightly the bearing runs is controlled by two cone-shaped pieces of metal that screw into the middle of the ring, pushing the balls outward against the ball race. Adjustment, therefore, is just a matter of slackening or loosening the cones.

First you should check whether adjustment is needed. Lift each wheel off the ground in turn and hold it by the rim at its highest point. Now move your hand sideways and see whether the wheel wobbles at the bearing. The most expensive hubs – Campagnolo and the best Shimano – should have no movement at all. At the same time, the wheel should revolve under its own weight, turning because the valve or the rim weld is heavier than the rest of the wheel.

If there's no wobble and the wheel turns smoothly, no adjustment is needed. In cheaper hubs, a barely perceptible amount of movement is not only permissible but even essential, to cope with any tight spots in the bearing.

If you look at the hub ends, you'll see a slender locknut and, inside it, a wider ring with two flats cut into it. On some hubs there's an adjustable cone on both sides, on others it's on only one side. Slacken the lockring with a thin cone spanner. Now put the spanner on the cone flat and turn it clockwise or anti-clockwise according to the adjustment. Make the same adjustment on the other side if necessary. Be careful to see that you're turning the cones the right way.

Unless the wheel is very slack, only the gentlest adjustment will be needed. Do it a little at a time, checking the wobble in the wheel each time. When you've got it just right, put one spanner on the cone flat to stop it turning, and then use another spanner to tighten the locknut.

Now check the wheel again. Unless you're very lucky, you'll have tightened the cone slightly as you turned the lock. As long as you didn't overdo it, this is easily rectified. This time hold the locknut steady and slacken the cone off as much as it'll go. That way you'll both slacken the cone a little and tighten it against the lockring.

Remember that you can't overdo this technique because if you leave the cone too loose, the whole assembly will become dangerously loose in less than a mile.

GEARS

Adjusting hub gears

Hub gears are made to need very little adjustment, and that in turn means that there's very little you can do. Problems come usually from the stretching of the gear cable. The gear lever then can't take up enough slack to pull the mechanism through the hub.

If you look at it, you'll see that on a Sturmey Archer gear the cable's connected via a slim, threaded rod to a small toggle chain that disappears into the hub. The threaded rod can be screwed into the end of the gear cable so that you tighten or loosen the wire. The thing to look for is the marked link in the toggle chain, or the larger end connection in it. This, when the gear is in its neutral position (second in three-speed gears) should be level with the end of the hub.

Everything from here is experiment. The exact point isn't hard to find, but it's not very tolerant. Tighten or slacken the cable each time by just a smidgeon and within a couple of moments you'll have got it just right.

Remember, by the way, that it's quite normal for the pedals to revolve idly when you push the bike.

Hub gears are complex beyond belief. Some dealers will take them apart but most – and you too, perhaps – will send them back to Sturmey Archer at Lenton Boulevard, Nottingham (unless, of course, they're made by Shimano or one of the other firms that holds a small part of the market).

Adjusting derailleur gears

Derailleurs work by bending one way or the other. The top and bottom bits stay at the same angle and the middle oblong section collapses into a parallelogram. How far the oblong swings is controlled by two small screws. You can see which does what by pushing the lever forward and bringing the chain on to the smallest sprocket. One screw will now be much nearer the frame of the gear than the other. Indeed, the end should be touching the frame.

If the gear won't select the smallest gear, unscrew the adjuster a quarter turn at a time until it swings out far enough. If, on the other hand, it keeps throwing the chain off the end of the sprockets, tighten it a little.

Now select the biggest sprocket by pulling the lever back. The other screw will (or should) be touching the back of the frame. Slacken it if you can't locate the big sprocket, tighten it if the chain or the bottom of the gear keeps going into the spokes.

It should be possible to set up a gear so that it works immaculately. If you just can't get it right, it could be because the chain is old; or the sprockets are worn and slightly hooked (look at them side on and see how different the left-hand side of the U shape is from the right); or the gear itself is bent or worn; or the frame is damaged; or the hub needs to be shifted a little more to one side by moving the spacing washers across.

Try to get the adjustment right. If after all your efforts it doesn't work, take your bike to a lightweight dealer.

Derailleur gears aren't very tolerant of wear. The chain has to be $^3\!/_{32}$-rather than $\frac{1}{8}$-inch and you can't run a new set of sprockets with an old chain. The answer to your problems, if you haven't touched the bike in years, could be to replace both. The cost isn't considerable.

The front derailleur works on the same principle and with the same adjustments. In some ways it's both cruder and more difficult to adjust. Get it wrong and you not only throw the chain off the big ring but you jam it down the side of the crank and buckle the chain cage.

When you ride, by the way, you have to change gear by slightly under-changing as you move into a higher gear, slightly over-changing as you move into a lower one. It's a technique easier to master than to explain. You'll also have to trim the front-changer from time to time as you select top or bottom gears at the back.

CHAIN

Shortening or replacing a chain

For this you'll need a specialist gadget called a chain riveter. It's a small clamp with a handle and a screw-in device with a pin on the end. You locate the chain and tighten the pin on to the end of a rivet (the bit through the middle of the link) and carry on turning until the pin pops out. The chain will then fall to bits.

If all you want to do is remove the chain and throw it away, then that's all you need do. If you want to replace segments of the chain, you have to take a lot of trouble to push the pin almost as far as it'll go . . . but not all the way. Turn very gently and you'll feel a slight click and the resistance will lessen. Stop turning.

Remove the riveter, pull gently at the chain, and it should come apart with the tip of the pin still secured in the frame of the link.

To add or withdraw a few links is therefore just a matter of working out where to make the junctions. Note that links aren't all the same. They are wider and narrower by turn, so you have to chop or join the chain so that you're left with a male end to join to a female.

If the pin does drop out, it's the devil's own job to get it back in place. You can do it but you need a lot of patience, so try to get it right to start with.

And another hint: when you take out a pin which you plan to screw back, start from the spoke side of the chain and push the pin out towards you. You'll appreciate it when you come to the more difficult job of pushing it back in again.

Note that ⅛-inch chains are fitted to bikes without derailleur gears and are commonly joined by a clip link. All you have to do is prise the spring-clip open and remove it. Half the link will then slide free. That saves you at least half the job.

Derailleur chains can't take such a link because of the way they have to twist and turn and go through narrow gaps. But Madison sell what they call a Superlink, which they boast *will* run with derailleur gears. There are different models for standard and narrow derailleur chains (for once again there's no such thing as standardization, even in chains).

Madison's address in this instance is Floor 1, Unit 7, Oxgate Lane, Cricklewood, London NW2.

HEADSET

Adjusting your headset

The headset is the main steering bearing. There are ball races at the top and the bottom and you can see at least half of them, or at least their shiny (or rusty) outer bits. You don't have to adjust the bottom race. The locknut at the top, where the handlebar stem runs into the frame, does both ends.

First slacken the locknut at the top of the various bulges and rings that make up a headset bearing. Now tighten or loosen the biggest bulge of the set until the looseness disappears. Hold the bulge firmly and tighten the locknut down on to it. In the process you'll probably tighten the bearing a little more than you intended, so it does no harm to start the operation with the headset slightly slack.

Never over-tighten a headset. The bearing surface pits extremely easily and a pitted headset is fit only for throwing away. It's better to have one that's slightly too loose, even though in the end that will wear as well. The perfect but exceptionally expensive Campagnolo headset goes on for ever, but if you don't fit it perfectly in the first place you'll ruin it. Get a dealer to fit a new headset. There are two sizes in the first place, and it's essential that the inner bearing surfaces are exactly parallel. It takes a special tool, and possibly some filing of the frame, to do a perfect job.

CRANKS

Tightening or fitting cranks

Cranks fit in one of two ways: Steel ones are drilled at their broad end to take a cotter pin. The holes link up with slots in the bottom bracket spindle. The pin is then dropped through and its flat surface filed thinner until it will fall through sufficiently far for enough thread to appear at the other end to take a nut and a washer. Too little thread will strip as the nut turns tight.

Convention dictates whether the nut is dropped in from the top or the bottom of the crank, and this convention varies from country to country. In some places you'll find the nut's on top and elsewhere that it's the blank end. Whichever you choose, make sure you do it the same on both sides, or the cranks won't be parallel.

If the crank comes loose, it'll wear quickly and might eventually come right off. Tighten the cotter pin to stop the wobbling. If you can't tighten it further, replace it.

Alloy cranks don't have the drilling and they fit a different spindle. They push on to a square or splined axle and they're held in place by a large, spanner-headed screw that winds into the end of the spindle. It's important to make sure the two parts are put together dry, that there's no grease or dirt. The spindle ends aren't parallel and the crank will wedge itself into a force-fit as you tighten it.

Never hammer the crank into place, and don't use excessive force. You'll need either the tool supplied by the maker or a thin-faced socket spanner. Don't use more than six inches of leverage. Turn the fixing screw until you meet firm resistance. Give it one extra tweak and leave it at that.

You need specialist tools to remove the cranks. What you use depends on the maker, so ask the dealer's advice.

BRAKES

Adjusting your brakes

There are three ways to adjust your brakes. Major adjustments are by slackening the bolt that secures the cable to the brake and then holding the brakes closed on the rim. Pull the cable through tightly, using a pair of pliers, and re-tighten the cable clamp. With luck, residual slack in the system will let the brake blocks inch back off the rim to let the wheels turn.

Note that in centre-pull brakes (where the cable runs to a yoke spread across the brake, rather than to just one side), the adjustment is made to the bolt that holds the wire to the triangular cable support.

For all these jobs, you need three hands: one to hold the brake, one for the cable, one for the spanner. You'll be pleased to hear that shops sell a gadget called just that: a third-hand tool.

You can make minor running adjustments with the furled knut where the brake cable first touches the brake and, on some brakes, by an adjustment where the cable leaves the brake levers.

The cheaper your brakes, the harder it will be to adjust them. If they prove almost impossible to get right, or they won't centre themselves (however much you undo the main bolt and readjust the tension springs), buy a better set. Your life depends on them, after all, and cheap brakes aren't cheap for nothing.

I nearly didn't add, because it seemed so obvious, that you can make your brakes much better by replacing the blocks. They're held in shoes (ease them out with a screwdriver) which are held by the obvious nut. Do make sure you put the shoes back the way they came out. If there's an open end, it should be at the back so that the turning wheel doesn't push the blocks out. And the front of the block should touch the wheel fractionally before the back. If it doesn't, and especially if the back touches first, there'll be a dreadful squeal as you stop.

The long and winding road . . .

Index